Happy 25th b[...]

May the next 25 years be as much fun!

Love, as always,

Carole Mortimer

Dear Reader,

As I am a regular contributor to Harlequin Presents®, love and marriage are always in my thoughts. And this year, in particular, they will be very much in the forefront of my mind—in a personal sense because in April 1998 my husband, Steven, and I shall be celebrating our silver wedding anniversary, and because, coincidentally and most felicitously, Presents will be celebrating its twenty-fifth anniversary, as well.

For me, this naturally calls for a very special double celebration and as you read these special books, I hope that you will share in my pleasure and enjoyment in writing for Presents.

These books are especially dear to my heart, as they celebrate not just the freshness of new romance, but also the capacity of love—like the Presents line itself—to grow and mature into something that those who experience it know has no equal and certainly no satisfactory substitute.

Congratulations, Harlequin Presents®, on such a wonderful lineup of books, and for providing what must be the most loyal and enthusiastic readers any author could possibly have.

My love to you all.

Penny Jordan

Penny Jordan

PENNY JORDAN

Fantasy for Two

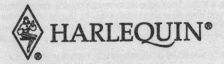

HARLEQUIN®

TORONTO • NEW YORK • LONDON
AMSTERDAM • PARIS • SYDNEY • HAMBURG
STOCKHOLM • ATHENS • TOKYO • MILAN • MADRID
PRAGUE • WARSAW • BUDAPEST • AUCKLAND

ISBN 0-373-11965-8

FANTASY FOR TWO

First North American Publication 1998.

CHAPTER ONE

MOLLIE'S pretty heart-shaped face was screwed up into a despairing glower, her topaz-flecked sherry brown eyes minus their usual sparkle as she studied the contents of her office diary. '2.30 p.m. drive to Edgehill Farm to interview the farmer's wife, Pat Lawson, re her special preserves recipe'. It wasn't exactly adrenalin-pumping, heartbeat-raising stuff, and working on a small-town local newspaper deep in the heart of rural England certainly wasn't what she had had in mind when she had been studying for her media degree, but realistically she knew that she was fortunate in having found a job at all. A good many of her peers had not done so and at least it was a start—a toe-hold on the career ladder which she hoped ultimately would lead to a much higher profile post, hopefully as either a newspaper or television journalist, covering all the important events of the day both at home and abroad.

It had been her parents, both of them careful and realistic in their outlook on life, and as different from Mollie with her vibrant and sometimes turbulent personality as it was possible to be, who had urged her to accept the job offer which had come up via one of her tutors at university.

'Dad, writing up weddings and country fairs for the local rag in some old-fashioned country market town isn't what I *want*,' Mollie had protested to her father when they had originally discussed the job.

'Maybe not,' her father had returned equably, giving her a small smile before adding dryly, 'You have to learn to walk before you can run, though, Mollie.'

'At least it's a job, darling,' her mother had chimed in. 'Although I wish you could have found something closer to home.'

Her parents lived in a comfortable London suburb and Mollie's new job was going to take her deep into a remote part of the West Country, a small country town on the coast which looked as though it would be more at home featuring in some TV historical drama than being the kind of place which could produce anything remotely newsworthy.

And Mollie, if she was honest about herself, had the kind of personality that dearly loved, even *needed* some kind of challenge, some kind of cause or person to champion, something or someone into which she could pour all the strong energy of her femininely fiery nature.

And she very much doubted that she was going to get that kind of stimulation writing about Mrs Lawson's family chutney recipes, even though she knew that it was the kind of thing that her mother, a very keen and skilled cook, would have fallen on with real pleasure.

She had only been in her new job—her first job—for just under a week, having spent her first weekend in Fordcaster settling into the small rented cottage which was to be her new home, and then her first three working days at the *Fordcaster Gazette*'s offices studying back copies of the paper and, as she had been instructed by the paper's owner and chief executive-cum-editor, 'absorbing the ethos' of his paper.

'You'll find Bob Fleury interesting to work for,' her tutor had told her when she had confirmed to him that she had accepted the job. 'He's a bit of an individualist, someone out of the common run—not entirely unlike yourself,' he had added wryly, watching as Mollie had struggled to suppress the desire to defend herself hotly against his subtle dig.

They had had several run-ins during her time at university. She was too impulsive, too inclined to react with her emotions and not her brain, he had often told her.

'Fleury—that's an unusual name,' she had managed to content herself with.

'Mmm...' he'd commented. 'He's got French blood. That part of the coast was heavily involved with smuggling during the years of the French Revolution, and the contraband they landed wasn't always merely inanimate objects.

'Bob's a traditionalist who, alongside seeing life in a very individual manner, can also be very set in his ways,' he had further told her. 'He believes there's a certain order to things and to people. Fordcaster is very much an archetypical English market town, and Bob represents its views and its determination to preserve the status quo.'

Mollie had listened ominously. The job was the absolute antithesis of everything she had hoped for when she had been studying for her degree, but she was realistic enough to know that it took more than a first-class degree to land the kind of plum job *she* had yearned for. She simply didn't have the kind of influence that would get her an entrée into the world she wanted to inhabit—at least not at this early stage in her career—and she suspected that her mischievous tutor was deriving great satisfaction from having persuaded her to accept a job which they both knew would demand far more of her emotional self-control and patience than it ever would of her degree skills.

'You can learn a lot from Bob, Mollie,' her tutor had told her more seriously before she'd left. 'Before he took over the paper—which, incidentally, has been in his family for several generations—he worked for a TV channel as one of their foremost foreign correspondents. What Bob doesn't know about that kind of reporting isn't *worth* knowing.

'Furthermore, many of the people he worked with in the field have gone on to fill very high-ranking posts within the corporation and the media in general.'

The smile he had given her then had done much to restore Mollie's faith, not just in him, but more importantly in herself. The job itself might not seem to offer much, he had subtly been telling her, but there were quite obviously potential opportunities that went with it that could promise a great deal.

Even so, she suspected that it was not going to be easy for her, working with Bob Fleury, and that she was going to have to do a good deal of biting on her tongue to keep her conflicting and often fiery independent views to herself.

They had already clashed once on the subject of hunting and Mollie suspected that there were going to be many other points of contention between them.

He must have some saving grace, though, because

his wife, Eileen, to whom he had introduced Mollie, was a surprisingly modern-minded woman with a decided twinkle in her eye and a warm smile that belied her quite formal country woman appearance.

Both Bob and Eileen were in their late fifties, but Eileen had some very up-to-the-minute ideas and their home, with its elegant simplicity, like Eileen herself, had impressed Mollie considerably.

It wasn't of Eileen, though, that she was thinking as she drove up a track which hopefully would lead to the farm.

She had already taken a couple of wrong turnings, the reason being that virtually all the land that surrounded the town was privately owned and subsequently its narrow lanes were bereft of any kind of sensible signposts.

Now, finally, she hoped she had found the right lane, but she was already running late for her appointment and Bob, as she knew, was a stickler for the old-fashioned kind of good manners which included being very strict about good timekeeping.

The sharp wind blowing across the Atlantic, up the English Channel and over the cliffs had tousled Mollie's hair when she had got out of the car earlier to check on her bearings, and now she pushed it irritably out of her eyes—a dark rich red heavy mass of glossy curls which, together with her small-boned frame, gave her an air of feminine fragility which she privately thoroughly resented.

She was a modern woman, strong-minded and independent, and she wanted to be treated as such. Her spirit and her personality more than made up for what she lacked in terms of physical strength and size.

She put her foot down a little harder on the accelerator. The lane was single track only, and not tarmacked, and she winced as her small car bumped uncomfortably over the deeper ruts.

Her mind on the coming interview, she neglected to hear or see anything of the battered Land Rover coming round the bend towards her, but fortunately its driver saw her and *he* brought *his* vehicle to an immediate brake-protesting stop which caused Mollie to realise her own danger and likewise apply her own brakes.

Her car stopped just inches short of the mud-spattered nose of his. Cursing under her breath at the delay, she saw the Land Rover's driver swinging open his door.

The last thing she needed now was to waste any more time. Angrily she pushed open her own door and got out. Whoever was driving the Land Rover wasn't the farmer. Bob had described him to her as a man in his sixties, and this man was nowhere near that. *Nowhere* near, she acknowledged, sucking in a sharp breath as she took a good look at him.

Tall—taller even than her father, who was just exactly six feet—and broad, extremely broad-shouldered, in the worn checked shirt he was wearing open at the throat to reveal a male vee of flesh disconcertingly shadowed by a soft sprinkling of very male-looking body hair.

His hair was black and very thick, his eyes an extraordinarily piercing shade of crystal-clear blue. They also possessed a certain steely look that for some obscure reason made her heart beat just a little bit faster and her chin go up as she fought down the odd mixture of nervousness and excitement that shot hotly through her veins.

She estimated that he was around thirty-two or three, almost a decade older than she was herself. But although his skin looked warmly tanned, suggesting that he spent a good deal of his time out of doors, and despite the fact that he was driving an extremely battered and shabby-looking Land Rover, and in defiance of the casual and well-worn clothes he was wearing, he had about him an air if not exactly of some dangerously good-looking predator, then certainly not one that fitted her mental image of a farmer.

He was far too sure of himself for one thing, far too arrogant and dominant in the way he approached her car and *her*, holding the door open for her in a gesture which, at face value, might seem courtly and polite but which Mollie assessed more darkly as a demeaning male act of aggression, an unspoken command to her to get out of her car.

If she hadn't already been doing so she would have firmly refused and remained where she was, but as it was she was already halfway out, and had very little option other than to complete the manoeuvre.

She wasn't going to allow him to think he had got the upper hand, though. *No way.*

Standing opposite him, she demanded aggressively, 'You do realise, don't you, that this is a private road?'

She could see from his expression that she had caught him off guard. He choked briefly and started to frown, his mouth hardening as he surveyed her grimly.

'A private road along which *you* were travelling too fast,' he retaliated smoothly.

He had a voice like rich, dark chocolate, Mollie recognised weakly. Very bitter rich, dark chocolate. She had always been susceptible to voices, and his was... She gulped and swallowed. His was...

Stop it, she warned herself severely. He isn't your type of man at all. You don't *like* dark-haired, dark-browed, shockingly handsome and seriously sexy men. You never have, and besides...

His lordly assumption of control plus his arrogant attitude, coupled with her own quick-to-take-fire emotions and her uncomfortable awareness that she *had* been driving just a bit too fast, had a predictably explosive effect on Mollie's temper.

'I was *not* driving too fast,' she contradicted him immediately—and untruthfully—and then added with what to her was perfectly reasonable logic, 'And besides, you were driving a Land Rover, so you must have seen me coming...'

'I did,' he agreed grimly, adding as though to underline his point, 'I stopped."

'So did *I*.'

The look he gave first the nose of her small car and then her made Mollie's face burn pink with angry colour.

'This is a private road over private land,' she began again. 'I have the permission of the owner to be driving along it—'

'You do?' She was interrupted softly.

'Yes, I do. I work for the *Fordcaster Gazette*.'

'Oh, you do, do you...?' he said gently, but Mollie was far too incensed to pick up on the subtle undercurrent of danger held in the softly spoken but very inflexible words.

'Yes, I do,' she agreed, recklessly ignoring the small warning voice trying despairingly to make itself heard, its protest drowned out by the hot, angry turmoil of her need to get the better of her foe as, tossing her head, she lied bravely, 'And anyway, the owner of this land happens to be a personal friend of mine.'

The dark eyebrows rose, the blue eyes suddenly looking coolly amused and holding an expression that was extremely cynical.

'I think not,' he corrected Mollie crisply, adding before she could say anything, 'You see, *I* happen to be the owner of this land, and this private road happens to be *my* private road.'

Mollie's mouth opened and then closed again. For sheer effrontery she had never met anyone like him.

'You're lying,' she told him fiercely once she had got her breath back. 'This road goes to Edgehill Farm, the *Lawsons'* farm.'

'To Edgehill Farm, yes, but it does *not* belong to the Lawsons; it belongs to me. The Lawsons are my tenants.'

'I—I don't believe you,' Mollie managed to stutter defensively.

'You mean you don't *want* to believe me,' he corrected her with a malign and very cold smile.

'Who are you anyway?' Mollie challenged him.

The cold smile became even colder, cold enough to make her shiver slightly, although she fought valiantly to conceal that fact from him.

'*I*,' he told her, pausing for effect and spacing each separate word carefully and precisely, 'am Peregrine Alexander Kavanagh Stewart Villiers, Earl of St Otel.'

Mollie gaped at him.

She had heard Bob Fleury mention his name in terms of revolting awe and admiration—to her at least; she knew he owned vast tracts of land not only locally but elsewhere in Britain as well, and that he was the holder of several ancient hereditary titles—none of which had impressed her in the least when she had heard Bob Fleury talking about him. But now…

She gulped and swallowed hard on her chagrin and the impulse to deny what he was saying and accuse him of deceiving her—something, some hitherto slumbering instinct, told her that would not be very wise.

She *couldn't* allow him to think he had totally routed her, though; it would not only go against the grain but would allow *him* to think that she was cowed, or even worse *impressed*, when the truth was that if anything the discovery of who he was had made her dislike him even more.

An earl. Well, *she* had no time for anything like that. *She* only accorded other people respect when she felt they *merited* it, and if he thought for one moment that just because he had flaunted his precious title…

'Well, I don't care *who* you are,' she told him defiantly, well beyond listening to any inner voice of caution or restraint. 'And if you think for one moment that I'm going to be intimidated by having you standing there like…like some Jane Austen character threatening to exercise some kind of…of droit du seigneur…'

The dark eyebrows shot up, the blue eyes gleaming with something that Mollie did not dare to try to ana-

lyse as he interrupted her suavely to say, 'I somehow
doubt that Jane Austen ever bestowed upon her male
characters any kind of rights of that nature... In fact,
I suspect she would have strongly disapproved of any
such suggestion.'

'Unlike you,' Mollie retorted dangerously.

'That depends... But since you seem so determined
to cast me in the role of villain and rake...'

Before she could guess what was happening he had
closed the distance between them and Mollie found
she was locked firmly against his body—a body
which felt far too robustly male for her feminine sus-
ceptibilities. He smelled of fresh air and the wind, and
beneath the protesting defensive hand she had put out
too late to ward him off she could feel the firm thud
of his heartbeat and the crisp roughness of the body
hair covering his skin.

He was all man. There was no doubt about that,
she acknowledged weakly.

Whilst she was trying to control her unwanted and
treacherous thoughts *he* was busily using one hand to
keep her secured against his body as the other cupped
her face and turned it to just the right angle for the
downward descent of his mouth. He was so skilful
that her last thought before his lips touched hers was
that it was a manoeuvre at which he was extremely
practised.

As though he had read her mind, she felt him whispering against her lips.

'I once had to play the villain in the village pan-
tomime...'

'I doubt there was much playing necessary,' Mollie
managed to mouth back through gritted teeth, before

the firm pressure of his lips on hers made further speech not just difficult but downright dangerous. To even try to open her mouth now, whilst it was being caressed so…so…by his, would be to invite…to…

'Mmm…' Giddily Mollie breathed a soft, appreciative sound of bliss as his lips stroked hers, and her own lips, her body, her ravished senses responded hedonistically to the delicious sensual mastery.

'Mmm…'

'Mmm…?'

To her chagrin Mollie recognised that he was repeating her soft sound of appreciation—*not* in confirmation of his own corresponding enjoyment of the kiss they were now sharing, but in fact as a question.

Immediately she stopped kissing him. Not that *she* had actually been kissing *him*, she tried to reassure herself as she primly firmed her kiss-softened lips against the provocation of the warmth of his breath and the tantalisingly gentle movement of his lips on hers… No, what *she* had been doing had quite simply and surely excusably been making an instinctive and automatic female response to the erotic mastery of a man who quite plainly knew far more about how to coax a woman into responding to him than was good for him—or for her.

Determinedly Mollie told herself that it wasn't disappointment that was chilling her blood as he allowed her to put some distance between them.

'How dare…?' she began shakily.

'How dare you, sir? Unhand me!' he finished for her promptly.

Mollie glared at him. Now he was quite definitely making fun of her.

'You had no right to do that,' she told him angrily, now that she was safely out of range of the strange and highly dangerous effect he had on her senses when he was close up against her. Talk about close up and personal—but she was not the sort of woman to be misled or deceived by her hormones. Just because he was skilled at the kind of kissing that made her feel as soft and squishy inside as—

'No? I thought you just said I had the right of droit du seigneur,' he reminded her softly.

He was laughing at her, Mollie decided—enjoying a very male-orientated joke at her expense. Now she really was angry.

'You do realise that what you've just done could be construed as sexual assault?' she began heatedly, only to have the fire really taken out of her argument.

'Is that why I'm going to have nail-marks on my arm from where you were holding onto me...?' he returned blankly.

Nail-marks. Mollie's eyes widened in a combination of embarrassment and fiery protest.

'I did not...' she began, only to stop as he started to roll up the sleeve of his shirt.

'You're in my way,' she told him instead, 'and I'm already late for my appointment with Mrs Lawson.'

'Pat won't mind,' he assured her easily. 'She'll be busy looking after her grandchildren.'

Pat Lawson might not mind but Bob Fleury would if news of her tardiness ever got back to his ears, Mollie recognised.

'If you won't move that...that thing,' she told him heatedly, tossing her curls in the direction of his Land Rover, 'then I'm just going to have to walk.'

As she started to turn determinedly away from him she thought she heard him laughing, but the next moment he was striding back to his Land Rover and climbing into it, throwing the engine into reverse and allowing her to drive her own car further up the lane to where there was a convenient passing place.

Arrogant brute, Mollie mentally slated him when she actually drove past, assiduously avoiding looking at him, her nose firmly in the air. And if *he* thought for one moment that *she* had actually enjoyed his odious and unwanted kiss, then…then…! Hot colour flooded her face as she missed a gear and heard the harsh. grating sound her car engine made in protest.

Half an hour later, standing in his study in the library of Otel Place drinking a coffee he had just made himself, Peregrine Alexander Kavanagh Stewart Villiers, or Alex as he was known to his close friends and associates, reflected ruefully on his recent run-in with Mollie and mentally admitted that he hadn't behaved very well.

His only excuse was that he had had a so-and-so of a morning, starting with a long-winded and petulantly plaintive telephone call from his stepmother complaining about the fact that her daughter—his stepsister—had announced that instead of completing her university course she had decided to take to the road with a band of travellers.

'Alex, you'll have to do something,' his stepmother had insisted. 'She's always listened to you.'

'Belinda, she's twenty and an adult,' Alex had wearily reminded her, forbearing to mention that the main cause of Sylvie's rebellion was her own mother, and the clinging possessiveness with which she had always treated her, refusing to allow her to grow up and be properly independent.

Sylvie, in his opinion, was a very unfortunate young woman, and his stepmother would have been the first person to complain if Alex had tried to interfere in their relationship—as had been proved in the past.

And then there had been an equally lengthy telephone call from the charitable trust, to whom his father had handed over the family's ancestral castle in a remote part of the Scottish Highlands. They had wanted to know the possible history of a tapestry which had just been discovered hidden behind a piece of Victorian panelling.

In the end Alex had had to refer them to the archivist of the family, a second cousin of his father's who was currently living in a house on another of the family's estates in Lincolnshire.

Like a good many other of the properties he owned, it was let out at a laughably nominal peppercorn rent. His financial advisors were constantly reminding him that by being so soft-hearted and housing not only several members of his family, including his stepmother, who lived in a very grand and expensive-to-keep apartment in London, but also various retired employees, and by paying for the upkeep of the properties they inhabited, he was depriving himself and, more importantly, the estate of income that was badly needed.

Very grimly Alex had had to remind them that so far as he was concerned there were more important

things in life than money—and far more important
duties and responsibilities.

The now retired employees living all but rent-free
in his properties had, as he had explained to the ac-
countants, served his family virtually all of their
working lives and deserved some comfort and security
in their retirement.

'But, my lord, surely you can see how advanta-
geous it would be if you were to revoke their tenancy
agreements and either let out the properties on
short-term leases at much higher rentals or simply sell
them.

'It isn't just a matter of the revenue you are losing
by allowing these people to live in them at such ridiculously low rents, there's the additional fact that
you are maintaining the properties for them. Only last
year you paid for a full row of terraced farmworkers'
cottages on your Yorkshire estate to be completely
modernised.'

'I'm sorry, but you're just going to have to accept
that I've made my decision so far as the tenancies are
concerned and I don't intend to change it,' Alex had
told them crisply.

The days when inheriting an earldom had meant
inheriting a life of ease and indolence were long
gone—if they had ever existed. Running large tracts
of land, not to mention the properties and farms that
stood on them, was, these days, sometimes a night-
mare of complex legislation and red tape coupled with
a never-ending battle to make financial ends meet.

Without the benefit of some very shrewd invest-
ments made by his great-grandfather, he doubted that
he would have been able to afford the luxury of keep-

ing the elegant Palladian mansion, Otel Place, which
had been his father's and was now his own principle
dwelling. His great-grandfather's money, though it
might not make him wealthy, had certainly made the
vital difference between his being able to keep most
of his inheritance and potentially having to sell off a
major part of it.

In fact, Alex now thought, the only bright spot in
an otherwise extremely fraught day had been the
run-in with his fiery, feisty redhead.

His? Momentarily he checked, and then frowned.
She had certainly been furious with him, and perhaps
with good reason, he acknowledged ruefully. He
could have set her right earlier and explained who he
was instead of helping her to dig the trap she had
hurled herself into so recklessly.

Had her eyes been topaz or gold? He closed his
own eyes—the smell of her perfume, light and tantalising, still clung to his shirt. She had felt good in
his arms, against his body, beneath his mouth—warm
and curvaceous, vibrant and alive.

He had known who she was, of course. Pat Lawson
had told him that she was coming to interview her
and he would probably have guessed anyway. Bob
Fleury had informed him of her appointment when he
had asked him if she could take up the tenancy of the
empty cottage in the square he owned down by the
river.

He *had* behaved rather badly, he acknowledged,
even if she had invited him to do it, and there had
certainly been no excuse for the way he had reacted
to her idiotic charge of him using any kind of right
to droit du seigneur. No, kissing her like that had been

wholly out of order—and wholly enjoyable. More, in fact, than merely enjoyable.

She had had an effect on him that... Hastily he reassembled his thoughts. He was thirty-three, for heaven's sake, and certainly a long way from allowing his hormones to dictate his behaviour to him.

No. He quite definitely owed her an apology and an explanation. He glanced at his watch. It was too late to call on her now, but he had to go into town later and he would call on her then to apologise.

CHAPTER TWO

'GOOD.'

Feeling highly satisfied with herself, Mollie put down the pages she had just been reading of the piece she had written following her meeting with Pat Lawson, pausing to study the view from her sitting-room window. Beyond her tiny front garden lay a well-maintained and very pretty town square, complete with its own private garden for which only the occupants of the houses around the square had keys.

The neat early Georgian cottages had, so Mollie had learned from Bob Fleury, a certain cachet to them, and she should consider herself very fortunate to be able to rent one of them.

The cottage certainly had a lot to recommend itself, Mollie had to acknowledge. Its location, with its long back garden backing onto the river and its frontage onto the small square, gave it an almost country feel, and its interior decoration showed not only good taste and a respect for maintaining period detail but a thorough awareness of the needs of modern life as well.

Her mother had been extremely impressed with the kitchen and bathroom when she and Mollie's father had driven down to Fordcaster with Mollie to help her get settled in.

'It's got a proper oven and not just a microwave,' her mother had approved. 'And everywhere's so clean.'

'Mmm... Apparently, according to Bob Fleury, the landlord is very particular about that sort of thing, and about who he takes on as tenants. Initially I've only been granted a lease for three months.'

'Well, I can see his point,' her mother had commented. 'If this was my house I certainly wouldn't want just anyone living here.'

Walking into the kitchen now, Mollie went to fill her kettle and make herself a hot drink.

Surprisingly Pat Lawson had proved to be extremely interesting to talk to, or rather to listen to, and in no time at all she had furnished Mollie not just with her great-grandmother's much prized recipe for her famous chutney but in addition a good deal of crisply informative and very witty background information about the history of the town, including some interesting facts about its foremost family—the Villiers of St Otel—both past and present.

'They go back right to the times of William the Conqueror,' she had told Mollie. 'The first earl came over from Normandy, although he wasn't an earl then, just one of William's knights. William gave him the earldom in return for his loyalty to him.

'Things haven't always been easy for them, of course. There was an earl beheaded in the time of Henry the Eighth, for supporting Anne Boleyn, and another during the Civil War; the most famous of them all, though, was probably the Black Earl—Rakehell St Otel, they called him. He made a fortune gaming in the clubs in London and then lost it again and ended up abducting an heiress so that he could marry her for her money.

'When, after six unsuccessful attempts to present

him with an heir, his countess finally gave birth to a much wanted son there was a rumour abroad that her child had been another girl and that she had been exchanged at birth for a boy child fathered on one of the serving wenches by her husband…'

Pat Lawson shook her head at this point, but Mollie was more interested in learning about the vices of the current Earl rather than his long-dead ancestor.

'What about the present Earl?' she pressed her, eager to gather ammunition against her adversary.

'Alex?' Pat responded, with an affectionate warmth and an easy familiarity which both surprised and displeased Mollie somewhat, causing her to scowl horribly and Pat to break off from what she had been about to say and enquire, 'Are you feeling quite well…?'

'Yes. Yes, I'm fine,' Mollie assured her hastily. 'Please go on. You were saying about Alex…about the Earl…'

Had Pat heard the angry note of censure and dislike in her voice as she'd said the word 'Earl'? Mollie shot the older woman a quick look. There was no point in alienating her by allowing her own feelings about the man to show, not when it was obvious both from Pat's doting tone of voice and the indulgent look on her face that *she* held a vastly different opinion of him.

'Oh, yes, Alex… He's had a hard time of it; there's no doubt about that.'

She paused whilst Mollie attempted to look duly sympathetic, although inwardly she was silently raging. 'A hard time of it'. Not from what she had seen, he hadn't. Oh, yes, she could really buy into that one.

'His father was killed hunting—which is one of the

reasons that Alex has banned it on his land—and his unexpected death left Alex with huge death duties to pay. Luckily he's managed to keep most of the land, even if he's had to cut down on staff.'

'I've read that more and more farmers and farmworkers are leaving the land,' Mollie commented.

An idea was beginning to take shape in her mind, the seeds of what she knew in her bones would make a truly controversial piece starting to germinate in the warm, receptive atmosphere of her own instinctive sympathy for the underdog and her equally instinctive dislike of Alexander, Earl of St Otel, and all that he stood for.

'Yes. Yes, some are.' Pat was agreeing sombrely with her. 'We've all had so many problems to face recently with there being so many food scares and new EC laws are coming into force.'

'I was thinking more specifically of the problems that occur when farmers and farmworkers who have devoted the whole of their working lives to their farms discover, when they come to retire, that they are expected to vacate properties which have probably been their homes for most of their lives. Tenanted farms and tied cottages...'

'Oh, yes, problems can and do occur,' Pat agreed readily. 'Often with tragic results.'

'Like the woman in the north of England who was evicted from the home she had lived in all her life after her husband's death, and expected to adapt to city life, living in a high-rise council block at eighty-two years of age,' Mollie supplemented for her, really beginning to warm to her theme. This was an area she had researched extensively as a student, and such injustices were very close to her heart.

'Yes, the law can be very unfair,' Pat acknowledged.

'Not the law, the landlords who implement it,' Mollie corrected her firmly. 'I know that the Earl is your landlord. I expect *he* owns a great deal of property, both locally and elsewhere.'

'Yes. Yes, he does, but...'

Mollie could see the headline now, hear the plaudits ringing in her ears as she exposed Alexander, Earl of St Otel, for the selfish, greedy monster that he undoubtedly was. Heavens, such a story might even attract the interest of a television documentary team, and then...

Not that she would ever write a single word motivated by self-interest, she told herself sternly. *That* simply wasn't her style. No, what she wanted to do was to draw people's attention to social injustices, to right wrongs, to slay dragons, and if one of those dragons should just happen to be the Earl of St Otel, then...then that only went to prove how right she had been to...to... Well, anyway, he had had no right to kiss her like that.

Thanking Pat for her time, she hurried back to the *Gazette*'s offices, where she diligently produced an article including the recipe for Pat's great-grandmother's famous chutney. But once she left work and got home she looked out her earlier research and seated herself in front of her own computer, where she set to work producing a far more controversial and explosive piece.

It was an exposé of the way wealthy and uncaring

land-owners treated their employees, and although she was scrupulously careful about not naming the Earl of St Otel—after all, she had nothing concrete in evidence against him yet—it was him Mollie had in mind as she worked on her article. He was, she had decided, the epitome of the greedy and uncaring land-owner, and a man too proud and arrogant, too selfish, to have a thought in his head for anyone other than himself.

Writing the article was one thing, she admitted, getting Bob Fleury to print it was quite another, but somehow she would find a way. She was determined. What she had to say, what she had to *reveal* and *unmask* about this nationwide issue was far too important not to be brought to people's attention.

The country's farmland was quickly becoming one vast mechanised food-production plant over which a small number of ever increasingly vastly wealthy individuals were acquiring total control—a business based merely on profits with no room in it for humanity nor for humans.

Sombrely Mollie watched now as a pair of geese flew over the river. Pat Lawson had mentioned during their conversation that there was a small nature reserve several miles away, the land and the small lake it included having been donated by a local philanthropist—some kindly elderly person, Mollie decided absently as she watched the geese disappear out of sight.

Alex grimaced as the Land Rover jolted out of a pothole in the road with a teeth-clenching rattle. He would dearly love to be able to replace it but he simply couldn't afford to. For him to spend money on a new vehicle for himself would mean that he would have to take money from some other project, such as replacing an essential piece of farm equipment or ensuring that all his tenanted cottages were properly repaired.

He frowned briefly and then made a determined effort to switch off from thinking about the problems that came from trying to turn ancient privilege and everything that went with it into a modern, self-financing environment fit to go forward into the new millennium—something which hopefully his children would inherit with serenity and joy instead of the grim near despair which he had had to take on with his inheritance following his father's unexpectedly early death. Death duties had been only the start of his problems, but hopefully they were now through the worst of things... Hopefully.

He looked ruefully at the small peace-offering on the passenger seat—a basket of peaches from the orangery that was the focal point of the house's kitchen garden. Built at the time of the original mansion, and modernised early on in the Edwardian era, its heating was provided by a complicated labyrinth of pipes and hot water fuelled by an ancient and temperamental boiler.

He himself had been on the point of deciding that the place would have to be emptied and closed down when a retired local gardener had come forward with the proposal that a local group of amateur enthusiasts take over not just the orangery and the succession houses that lined the south wall of the kitchen garden, but also the kitchen garden itself.

This collective, of which he himself was now a

part, in that he was an honorary member of their group, shared the produce which the garden gave. The peaches he had packed carefully in a basket surrounded by tissue paper were his share of this season's.

For reasons which he had no intention of going into, their lush promise reminded him very much of the person for whom his gift was intended. Their fruit would be sweet and juicy but with an explosive and challenging sharpness. Deftly he swung the Land Rover over to the side of the road and parked it.

Mollie frowned as she heard the knock on her front door. She wasn't expecting anyone. She had not had any time to make any friends in the town as yet, and virtually the only two people she knew were Bob Fleury and his wife.

Switching off the kettle, she went to answer the door. When she opened it her eyes widened in wary suspicion as she saw who was standing there.

'What do *you* want?' she demanded challengingly, before adding, 'If you've come to apologise…'

'I haven't,' Alex replied coolly. What was it about her, this five-foot-nothing bundle of aggressive womanhood with her tangle of curls and her amazingly coloured eyes, that somehow set his pulses racing and despite all his good intentions made him feel…made him react…?

'Then what *do* you want?' Mollie demanded.

Heavens, what was the matter with her? What was it about the man that made her behave so…so femininely…? She could actually feel her toes curling inside her shoes as she fought valiantly to control the dangerously awakening flood of awareness that swamped her as she stood there on her doorstep.

He represented everything she most disliked in a man, and yet here was her body telling her the opposite, luring her. Even more angry with herself than she was with him, Mollie took a step backwards, intending to close the door, but to her chagrin Alex had stepped inside before she could do so.

'How dare you? This is *my* house—' she began, only to have him cut her short.

'No, it isn't, it's mine,' he said cynically.

Mollie gaped at him.

'*You're* my landlord?' she guessed, determined not to be caught out the same way again.

'Yes, as a matter of fact I am,' Alex agreed. 'But...'

What on earth was going on? The whole situation was rapidly getting totally out of hand. He *hadn't* come here to argue with her, dammit. He had come to...

To Mollie, his arrival so soon after she had finished writing her article only served to add fuel to her already turbulent emotions.

'You might be able to browbeat and...and terrorise your other tenants, especially those unfortunate enough to owe their living to you, but I'm not—' she began, but Alex had heard enough. He had never known a woman get under his skin so quickly or so thoroughly, and of all the wrong-headed and totally unjust accusations he had ever heard hers certainly took some beating.

'Now just a minute—' he began, but Mollie was in no mood to listen to him.

'You're trespassing,' she told him dangerously. 'And if you don't leave immediately I shall...'

Alex, she realised, wasn't listening to her. He was staring at the article she had so recently finished printing out and which she had left on the table in front of which he was now standing.

Attached to the front of it was a boldly handwritten note bearing his name, which she had underlined thickly, adding three heavily drawn exclamation marks. His earlier frown had become a black-browed scowl, and the very air around them in the small room seemed to have taken on a thunderous, sulphurous atmosphere.

'Would you mind explaining to me what the hell this is supposed to be?' she heard him demanding slowly as he spaced out each separate word with infinite care and ice-cold fury.

'I should have thought it was obvious. It's an article I've just written on the dreadful and iniquitous way farmworkers are treated at the end of their working lives...' Mollie responded, determinedly tilting her chin as she met his furious glare head-on. She refused to give way either to his very obvious ire or her own quivering inner reaction of excitement and alarm at what she had caused.

'Are you trying to imply that *my* farmworkers are badly treated?' Alex asked her.

Mollie's chin lifted even higher.

'And if I *am*,' she demanded. 'Are you going to deny that you have turned people out of their homes to make room for new, younger employees?'

'Yes, I am.'

Mollie blinked. She hadn't been expecting such a

categoric and totally barefaced misappropriation of the truth.

'You're lying,' she told him positively.

Alex couldn't believe what he was hearing. Her accusations were so ludicrous and so far off the truth that if they hadn't been such a damned insult, and if she hadn't been so positive that she was right, then he would have been more inclined to laugh than get angry. However…! Clenching his jaw, he told her ominously quietly, 'I do not *lie*.'

'Liars always say that,' Mollie replied sweetly.

'This is impossible. *You* are impossible,' Alex retorted. 'And if you think for one moment that anyone with a shred of intelligence is going to publish this…this *rubbish*, then…'

As he spoke he was reaching for the article. Instinctively Mollie acted to protect it, to stop him reaching out. Alex got there first, crumpling up the sheets in his fist as Mollie tried to tear his fingers from around them.

Instinctively Alex started to turn away from her, but Mollie, who had reached up on her toes, stretching her body out precariously to try to retrieve the article, started to lose her balance, causing Alex to do the only possible thing he could do.

Mollie's small, instinctive cry of alarm was smothered against the solid wall of his chest as he dropped the article and reached instead for her.

'Let me go. *Let me go*,' Mollie demanded, hammering hard against his chest with two small bunched fists, oblivious to the fact that but for his chivalrous gesture she would probably have been lying ignominiously in a heap at his feet instead of being held protectively and safely against the marginally less ungiving hardness of his body.

Both the floor and his muscles might be equally tough, but *her* body was certainly reacting very, very differently to the muscles than it would have done to the floor. The quivering, jelly-like shakiness which had invaded her limbs was certainly not the kind of reaction she could ever remember having after coming into contact with any kind of inanimate object. Come to think of it she couldn't remember ever having experienced such a mind-boggling reaction to coming into contact with anything or any*one* at any time in her whole life before. It really was too bad of her body to react to him in this wretchedly puerile fashion, she told herself sternly. He was, after all, *only* a man.

'I hate you. Let me go at once,' she told him furiously—just to make sure that he understood that the by now openly visible trembling of her body meant nothing whatsoever, and that if he was unwise enough to think that it did...

'Likewise,' she heard him telling her through gritted teeth.

So, given that both of them had expressed their dislike of one another so plainly, why was it that they were now locked in one another's arms, kissing like a pair of starving lovers who had been apart for centuries?

Mollie had no idea. She only knew that the angry, passionate, devouring kisses their mouths were hungrily demanding from one another seemed to *feed* the need she could feel boiling up inside her rather than satiate it.

She had never dreamed that she could feel like this about *anyone*, that she could desire anyone so passionately, so intensely, so…so insanely…and so compulsively that she knew that if she didn't somehow find a way to put a brake on what she was experiencing it wouldn't be Alex who might be tearing off her clothes in order to make love to her, but *she* who was tearing off *his*.

That was what he did to her… That was how he made her feel. It wasn't love; it wasn't even lust… What exactly it was she couldn't even begin to put a name to… She only knew it was something explosive. Something dangerous… Something over which she was totally without control—a starving, famished, aching need that twisted tormentedly through her as she alternately pushed him away and then pulled him closer, her mouth biting hungrily at his, her lips closing around his hot, hard tongue, her hips grinding into his as he grasped them and held her, *his* body mirroring the fiercely sensual movements of hers.

She could feel his arousal and her own body ached and pulsed in response. A series of frantic mental images crowded her brain, sharply clear flashes…images of the two of them entwined together, their bodies naked, his skin glistening with sweat, sleek, tanned, roughened with soft dark hair, hers paler, softer but no less aroused.

She could feel her nipples hardening, thrusting against her clothes. Her teeth worried at his lower lip. She could hear him groan and felt his answering passion in the way his hands moved over her body, shaping her, moulding her, cupping her breasts, holding them in such a way that she literally shook with aching need.

She could feel herself starting to moan as the force of it possessed her body; a reciprocal shudder racked Alex's body, and the sound he made, a low, raw groan, reverberated through her as their mouths fused hotly together. And then, abruptly and shockingly, Mollie felt Alex lift his mouth from hers and firmly push her away from him.

Instinctively she resisted, her senses so thoroughly aroused and aching for him that she couldn't bear to let him go. And then, thankfully, before she could make a complete fool of herself, sanity and common sense came to her rescue, allowing her to shrug off the hands still clasping her forearms and to assume an expression of furious anger as she demanded huskily, 'How dare you…? How *dare* you—?'

She broke off as she caught sight of the basket of peaches Alex had brought in with him, thankful to have something other than him on which to focus her attention and her chaotic emotions. 'And just where did those come from?' she asked aggressively.

'I brought them with me,' Alex told her curtly. 'They're home-grown—from the orangery.'

He was still trying to understand just what had prompted him to behave in such an uncharacteristic fashion. He was sexually experienced enough to recognise the potential destruction that could be caused by emotions, sensations as explosive as those he had just experienced, but there had been a feeling, a need within him when he had held Mollie in his arms which had gone far, far beyond any mere desire for sex.

He could tell, too, that even though she was trying valiantly to hide it from him she had been as caught off guard, as unable to control what had happened as he had been himself.

The last thing he needed right now was to get involved with a woman, a situation like this one. He had enough problems in his life already. More than enough.

'The orangery,' Mollie repeated bitingly. 'And how many poor souls have you had to evict from their homes to pay for that kind of luxury, I should like to know?'

'I'm sure you would,' Alex agreed.

'These peaches are rotten—rotten because they've been grown and fed on human misery,' Mollie told him dramatically, tilting her head proudly as she added, 'It's all there in my article—the way that people, *men* like you—'

'You can't publish what you've written...' Alex began to tell her, intending to warn her that she had got her facts totally wrong, but before he could finish Mollie immediately interrupted.

'You can't intimidate *me*,' she told him passionately.

Alex opened his mouth to tell her that intimidating her or anyone else had never entered his mind, nor was it ever likely to do so, and that essentially at heart he was a pacifist, a man who applauded and worked for harmony, a man who *respected* the views and feelings of others. But instead, to his own bemusement, he heard himself saying in a passably threatening male growl, 'Don't be so sure.'

The tiny quiver of sensation that shivered through

Mollie's body as she heard him wasn't entirely based on fear, but, wisely, she had no intention of investigating just why the look in his eyes and the tone of his voice should generate within her a feeling not unlike the delicious excitement she had experienced as a child when engaging in some activity which she had known to be forbidden.

'Typical,' she responded contemptuously to Alex instead, with a provocative toss of her head. 'But you don't frighten me.'

Grimacing to himself, Alex turned away from her and headed for the front door.

'Maybe not,' he muttered to himself under his breath as he angrily yanked the door open and strode through it. 'But you sure as hell frighten me.'

No wonder he had stormed off like that, Mollie crowed in mental triumph as she firmly slammed the door after him. He had known she had him routed, that she couldn't be bullied or pushed or cowed, as *he* had no doubt expected.

Walking back into her living room, she absent-mindedly picked up one of the peaches and bit deeply into it. The fruit was luscious and sweet, with a taste that made her close her eyes in momentary sensual bliss.

'Mmm...yummy...'

She had virtually finished the peach before she remembered what she had said to its donor. Well, never mind, she wasn't one to look a gift-horse in the mouth, she told herself stoutly. How many peaches were there exactly in that basket? Three more... Well, it would be wasteful not to eat them, an insult to whoever had taken such care in growing and nurturing them...

The next day, standing in Bob's office whilst she waited for him to finish reading her article, Mollie was still seething over her run-in with Alex. How *dare* he threaten her? He was typical of his type: rich, arrogant, completely oblivious to the thoughts and feelings of others.

But it was his threat to her article that concerned her the most and possessed her thoughts, not what had gone before it. In fact that kiss they had shared, and her own regrettably insane and inadmissibly intense response to it, was something she simply wasn't prepared to dwell on or give any kind of credence to by thinking about it. Everyone was permitted the odd small aberration.

She had been under stress, caught off guard. *He* had no doubt expected her to reject him, and would have enjoyed having her behave in what to him would have been a predictably female and victimish way. By kissing him back, by showing no fear, she had shown him that she was *not* so predictable, so easily readable, that she was *not* the kind of woman who was going to be overawed or daunted by him.

She was no fool. Of course there would be members of her sex who would be silly enough to be taken in by his good looks and by the aura of success and maleness that clung to him, but *she* was most certainly not one of them.

Bob had reached the end of her article. He put it down and removed his spectacles, and then frowned as he told her baldly, 'We can't print this. You do

realise that people locally will assume that this landlord you refer to is Alex, and—?'

'And because he happens to own half the county
no one is allowed to say or write anything that might
show him up in his true colours? Is that it?' Mollie
interrupted him hotly.

Bob Fleury's frown deepened as he looked at her.

His grandfather on his mother's side had been a
Scot, and Bob had inherited some of his dourness and
his cautious carefulness, which balanced his more un-
predictable French trait. Now, as he placed both his
hands on his desk and studied Mollie, he chose his
words very carefully.

She was such a fiery young thing, with so much
still to learn, but he liked her. She had spirit and, just
as important, she genuinely cared about her fellow
human beings. He had no time for these cynical and
worldly young people who seemed bored with their
lives before they had really begun.

'Is that what you think—that Alex is the kind of
landlord you've written about in this article?'

'Well, isn't he?' Mollie challenged him.

'No,' Bob told her promptly and firmly. 'I've
known Alex all his life and there is no way he would
ever treat his tenants badly. In fact, one of the first
things he did after his father's death was set about
raising enough money to ensure that those who had
worked for his father and were close to retirement
could be securely housed when they reached retirement age.

'He had to fight like the devil to get his plans past
the local planning committee as well. Simply allowing
people to stay on in the often remote cottages they

had occupied during their working lives wasn't enough for Alex. No. What he did was bring in an architect and instruct him to design purpose-built units suitable for independent elderly people to live in.'

Now it was Mollie's turn to frown.

'Anyone can make plans...promises...' she began, but Bob shook his head, forestalling her.

'Alex did more than that,' he told her firmly. 'Wherever he owns an estate he has financed the building of a small development of these units, close to all the local amenities and complete with resident wardens and facilities for the disabled. He's even financed a nursing home for those ex-employees who can no longer manage to live by themselves.'

'But Pat said—' Mollie began, only to have her boss cut across her objection a second time.

'There's no way Pat Lawson would ever criticise Alex,' he told her. 'She thinks the world of him.'

Mollie looked away. It was true that Pat Lawson had never actually mentioned Alex by *name*, she acknowledged unhappily, but she had assumed when the older woman had agreed with her own comments that she had known that Mollie was obliquely referring to him.

'No, I'm sorry,' she heard Bob telling her, and he very firmly tore her prized article in two, and then two again, before depositing the pieces in his waste-paper basket.

Then he asked her, 'Did you get Pat's recipe?'

'She's young and enthusiastic,' his wife reminded him gently later in the day, when they were having lunch together at the White Swan. The pub had originally been a coaching inn, and since it was owned by Alex it had escaped any kind of themed modernisation and was still very much a traditional English pub, with proper English food including Bob's favourite steak and ale pie.

'She needs something she can get her teeth into,' Eileen added. 'She doesn't want to write about recipes and knitting patterns.'

'Maybe so, but I can't understand her—to write something like that about Alex of all people...' Bob said, shaking his head. 'I told her one of the first things any journalist worth their salt has to learn is to get their facts right. I mean *Alex*... I can't think what's got into the girl. She seems to have taken a real dislike to him.'

'She needs a crusade...' Eileen told him wisely, before adding firmly, 'You know what the doctor said about your cholesterol level. Why don't you have the chicken salad?'

Mollie could feel her ears burning hotly as she walked through the *Gazette*'s main office. No doubt everyone had heard Bob rubbishing her article this morning. Well, she didn't care what Bob said; she knew, she just knew that there was no way that Alex was as white as he liked to be painted. After all, she had first-hand knowledge of just how badly he could behave when he wanted to, hadn't she?

A brief touch on her arm made her jump. She turned her head to find Bob's secretary smiling at her.

'I was just going out for lunch,' she told Mollie, 'and I wondered if you'd like to come with me.'

'I'd love to,' Mollie accepted gratefully. With the

exception of Lucy, the secretary, all the other members of the *Gazette*'s staff were of a similar age to its owner, and although she was a girl who had never found a problem in meeting and making new friends, and one who, moreover, enjoyed her own company, she had begun to feel slightly isolated and alone since moving to the town.

Bob had just kissed his wife goodbye and was about to walk out of the White Swan when he was hailed by an old friend—the chief inspector of the town's police force—who, he saw, was frowning grimly.

'Something wrong?' he asked casually.

'You could say that,' he was told. 'We've just been put on alert. It seems we've got a convoy of travellers heading out this way.'

'Travellers?' Bob questioned slightly bemused.

'Yes. You know—hippies, New Agers...' the chief inspector explained briefly. 'They pitch up and make camp with their caravans and their lorries and cause the devil's own kind of problems. If they do decide to make camp locally I'll have every farmer for miles around on my back wanting me to get rid of them, not to mention the calls we'll be getting from anxious parents worrying about the possibility of them selling drugs and generally causing problems.

'I've been trying to track Alex down,' he added.

'It's more than likely to be his land they settle on if they *do* settle locally, so it will be up to him to seek what legal remedies he can to move them on.'

'What makes them do it, I wonder...?' Bob mused. 'I mean why...why decide to live outside society instead of within it?'

'You're the journalist, not me. Although most of them would tell you that they have chosen to create their *own* society...'

'Mmm...'

Having refused his offer of a drink, Bob made his way back to the *Gazette*'s offices. If the travellers did decide to settle locally his readers would want to know exactly what was going on. Not, from what he had just heard about them, that any of these young people were likely to confide to *him* what their plans were. A thought suddenly struck him.

'She needs something she can get her teeth into,' his wife had told him about his new employee... 'She needs a crusade...'

After a sandwich and an enjoyable chat with Lucy, which had included an invitation for Mollie to join Lucy and some of her friends on a ramble the following weekend, followed by a meal at a local pub, Mollie returned to the *Gazette*'s offices feeling much more cheerful. But her heart sank a little bit as, before she could reach her desk, Bob appeared and asked her to step into his office.

'New Age travellers are coming here and you want me to interview them?' Mollie asked him excitedly when he had explained what was going to happen. This was more like it. This was the kind of human interest story she could *really* get her teeth into.

'The *Gazette*'s readers are going to want to know what these people are about, why they can't stay in their own homes. Don't they realise the havoc they cause, the damage they do to local crops and livestock?' Bob was demanding critically, pursing his lips.

Mollie could tell exactly what kind of article *he* wanted her to write, but there were always two sides to every story.

'We don't know yet if these people do intend to pitch camp locally,' Bob was reminding her. 'With any luck they won't, but—'

'Where are they now? Does anyone know?' Mollie interrupted him excitedly.

'Well, they're travelling this way, from the north. The police are keeping an eye on them, but apparently there's not an awful lot they can do.'

Mollie quickly drew a brief mental map of the town's infrastructure. That meant they must be travelling on what had once been the London road. Even if they decided *not* to pitch camp locally, it would still be worthwhile interviewing them, finding out how they lived, what had made them take to the road in the first place.

'I could drive out to meet them and see if I can do some interviews,' she suggested, holding her breath until Bob had given a brief grunt of assent.

Alex received the news of the travellers' imminent arrival with far less enthusiasm.

He was not antagonistic towards their way of life, nor to them, and in many ways felt extremely sympathetic towards them, but... But he was also a land-owner and a landlord. He knew the havoc their arrival could cause, and the friction which could develop between them and their unwilling hosts. What he couldn't quite understand, though, was why on earth they should have picked on Fordcaster. They were a small, quiet backwater of a town, well off any of the main arterial routes.

The police had already advised him to get in touch with his solicitor and set in motion what legal remedies he could to evict them, should they decide to settle. Unwillingly he reached for the phone. He didn't like having to turn away anyone who was in need—it went against his whole ethos and nature—but he also owed a duty to his tenants.

Reluctantly, he dialled the number of his solicitor.

Mollie saw the police car first, strategically parked where its driver could monitor the traffic passing along the main road.

Impulsively she stopped and parked her own car, getting out to go and talk to the driver.

'I'm from the *Gazette*,' she told him. 'My editor wants me to interview the travellers, find out what their plans are…'

The policeman gave her a distinctly unimpressed look.

'That's something we'd all like to know,' he told her dryly. 'Including my wife. I've already worked two hours over my shift…'

'How long do you think it will be before they reach town?' Mollie asked him.

'No idea—' he began, and then stopped as his radio crackled into life.

'They've turned off onto the B4387,' she heard the unseen speaker telling him over the radio. 'But stay where you are just in case they double back.'

Quickly memorising the road number, Mollie hurried back to her own car. She had a map and it only took her a few minutes to find the B road she was looking for. So far as she could see it was a narrow, meandering route which bypassed the town and wandered alongside several fields and a small wood before turning back on itself to meet up with the main road again on the other side of town.

Frowning, Mollie rechecked the road number. From the map she could see no reason why the travellers should want to take such a route. It didn't seem to go anywhere and she suspected that if they chose to do so the authorities could block both ends of it and effectively contain the travellers there.

Perhaps she had got the number wrong? There was only one way to find out.

CHAPTER THREE

'THEY'VE done what?'

Alex pushed his hand into his hair as he listened to what the chief inspector was telling him.

'Damn,' he cursed. 'That road borders Hesketh Wood. We've a pair of kestrels who nest there and we're trying to get the area listed as a protected area of outstanding natural beauty.

'No, I appreciate that you can't do anything,' he agreed. 'But why the hell have they chosen to go down there? That road goes nowhere, and unless you knew it you'd never...'

Shaking his head, Alex replaced the telephone receiver.

Hesketh Wood belonged to him, although it was on land farmed by one of his tenants. Over the last three years, between them he and Ranulf Carrington, and many volunteers, had spent a good deal of time and money cleaning out the lake within the wood and introducing native fish into it, as well as carefully replanting some damaged areas of woodland with natural broad-leaved trees.

It was home to at least three separate sets of badgers that Alex knew of, and the remnants of the pheasants his father's gamekeeper had once reared for shooting had made their home there; the local primary schools organised days out there in the summer, for picnics and nature walks for their pupils, and *Country*

Life had run an article about the place the year before last, when Alex had first started getting results on bringing it back to life.

They had planted a carefully chosen selection of woodland ferns and flowers in it and the kestrels, which had nested there for the first time this year, had successfully taught their young to fly. They had high hopes that the red squirrels they had released there would breed too.

The last thing, the very last thing he wanted was to have all the careful ecological planning they had made disrupted by the arrival of anyone who was not aware of or sympathetic to what they were trying to achieve.

The police had informed him that the travellers had already turned onto the road that went past the wood. With any luck they would simply be using it to bypass the main road and any police roadblocks; the best thing he could do was wait and see what happened.

But the road was narrow and meandering, seldom used since the opening of the new bypass and travelled only by locals.

Reaching for his car keys, he headed for the front door.

Mollie was just about to turn round and drive back when she found the travellers.

The convoy had come to a standstill, waiting for the trailers, caravans and lorries at its head to make their way through a farm gate and along a country track which disappeared into woodland.

A young woman clad in a waxed jacket and jeans stood by the gate, apparently directing operations, and Mollie, who had travelled in the opposite direction, parked her car and got out, hurrying towards the woman.

'Hello. I'm Mollie Barnes,' she introduced herself. 'I work for the local paper.'

The girl, who after a brief scowling look at Mollie had turned her head away from her, swung round, giving her an amused and cynical look. Too cynical for someone who looked as though she couldn't be much more than twenty.

'The *Gazette*. Yah... Really big time...'

Her cut-glass accent and bored upper class manner were not what Mollie had been expecting—neither was the Versace logo on the designer jeans she was wearing. But, mentally chiding herself for her own inappropriate reaction to the girl, Mollie firmly dismissed her instinctive wariness. Where, after all, was it written that a New Ager should not wear Versace? Mollie asked herself firmly.

'Who sent you here? Old Fleury?' the girl guessed. 'Trust him. I suppose he's frothing at the mouth and all ready to stir up the locals against us.'

The girl was certainly well informed about the town and its inhabitants, Mollie recognised, moving back from the gate as a large and unwieldy lorry made its way through it, crashing into one of the gateposts and sending the wood splintering to the floor.

'Aren't some of these vehicles a bit too heavy for an unmade-up road?' she asked the girl uncertainly.

'They'll make it into the wood,' she told her, shrugging her shoulders. 'Even if some of them have to get a tow. But whether or not they can get out again... Not that it matters. We'll be here now for some months.' She gave Mollie a challenging smile. 'Now there's something for you to tell your readers—something that will really set them twittering.'

Mollie looked uncertainly at the land in front of them. The wood looked so pretty and unspoiled, and she winced as one of the caravans swayed into a vulnerable young sapling. There couldn't possibly be any fresh water supply or sanitation here, and from what she could count there were at least a hundred and possibly more vehicles.

'Look, we have to live somewhere,' the girl told her, obviously guessing what she was thinking, adding challengingly, 'Have you any idea how it feels to be treated like a…a leper wherever you go, to be rejected and…and vilified? We all have a right to live normal, decent human lives and that's all we ask. All we want is to be left alone, to live as we choose to live.'

She sounded so passionate and sincere that Mollie's sympathies were instantly stirred. She was right. Everyone deserved the right to control their own lives.

'We're not doing anything wrong,' the girl continued passionately, sensing that Mollie's sympathies lay with her.

'It *is* private land,' Mollie felt obliged to point out objectively.

'Maybe now, but by what right?' the girl demanded fiercely.

'Once, all this land—' she gestured with a big sweep of her arm to encompass not just the small, pretty wood but the farmland which surrounded it as well '—belonged to the *people*. They—*we* are the ones who should have rights over it, but it was stolen from us, taken by force of arms.'

She clearly believed in her cause, Mollie could see,

and despite her initial reservations she could feel herself warming towards the younger girl, even if she felt a little intimidated by the watchful presence of the man who was standing a couple of feet away from them, listening to her.

'But now we'll be the ones doing the fighting to reclaim what is rightfully ours,' the girl went on, telling Mollie, 'Historically, this place was a regular stopping site for gypsies, but in the eighteenth century, when the land was enclosed, the gypsies were driven off, their livestock killed, their men put in prison and their women raped. It's our right to be here and no one is going to move us on until we're ready to go, and that won't be for a while.'

'That's right,' the man agreed softly, coming over to join them, his arm going round the girl and his hand reaching out to caress her in a gesture of such intimacy that Mollie found herself instinctively looking away from them.

It wasn't that she was prudish; far from it. It was just that…that there was something about his attitude towards the girl that struck a wrong note somehow, and even though she was smiling at him Mollie could see how she had tensed against his touch.

It was plain from the orders he was shouting out to the caravan of vehicles still pouring in through the gate that he was if not *the* leader then certainly one of the leaders of the convoy. But, unlike the girl, he did not have an upper-class accent, and there was something about the sharp, narrow-eyed look he was giving her that left Mollie feeling oddly chilled. He was not, she suspected, a man it would be wise to cross.

'You say you intend to stay here over the winter,' she commented, turning back to the girl. 'How will you manage to live? This isn't a designated site; it doesn't have running water or...'

'There's a standpipe in the field on the other side of the wood,' the girl told her knowledgably, 'and once he realises he can't move us on then it will be up to the land-owner to make proper provision for us—bring in Portaloos and showers. If he doesn't...'

She gave a small shrug and then told Mollie, 'But he will. I know—'

'Sylvie knows him well. Don't you, my lovely?' her boyfriend interrupted her with a knowing look.

'I should do,' she agreed with a small toss of her head. 'After all, I lived with him for four years...'

Four years?

Four years. Mollie tried to conceal her shock.

The girl didn't look any more than twenty or twenty-one at the very most, which meant that if, as she seemed to be implying, she and whoever owned the land had been lovers she could only have been around sixteen at the time she had begun to live with him.

A small group of men and women were approaching the gate from the wood and they stopped as they reached Mollie's companions, one of them turning to the man to tell him, 'We've parked up and now we're off into town to Social Security to make sure they get the giros sorted out... Who's she?' he added, jerking his head in Mollie's direction and then spitting out the gum he had been chewing.

Trying not to betray her distaste, Mollie answered

him herself, explaining, 'I'm a reporter with the local paper...'

'A reporter...?' the man mimicked tauntingly. 'And with the local paper... My, my... When do you reckon the TV people will be down here?' he asked the other man, turning his back on Mollie. 'We need to get public opinion on our side, let people know that we're here and that we intend to stay here. You know the kind of conniving bastards who own places like this. He could try to bring in people to shift us before news gets out that we're here.'

'Just let him try.'

This time it was the girl who was speaking, her face flushing and her eyes darkening with obvious emotion.

What had happened between them? Mollie found herself wondering sympathetically. Had *she* left him, or had *he* grown tired of her and thrown her out? What kind of man was he, anyway, to seduce a young girl of sixteen? And where were her parents, her family, the people who should have been guarding and protecting her?

'Oh, he'll try all right,' her boyfriend announced softly. 'But when he does we'll be ready for him...'

Mollie frowned. Her instincts told her that there was more to this situation than met the eye, and that the young woman facing her had some kind of personal grudge against whoever owned this land.

If so, that was between her and him, she reminded herself firmly. *She* was here simply to report on the arrival of the travellers and the effect they were likely to have on the local community.

'Be a great place to stage a rave,' one of the small group at the gate remarked.

A small frown touched Mollie's forehead.

'Nah…it's too remote,' another of them remarked.

Out of the corner of her eye Mollie noticed a thin young girl approaching the couple she had been talking with. She was clutching a crying baby, and a toddler with a runny nose was clinging to her jean-clad legs.

She said something to the man that Mollie couldn't catch, and when he shook his head she started to tug pleadingly on his arm as she began to cry.

'But I'll get the money. You know that…' Mollie heard the girl protesting as he started to push her away.

She'd get the money for what? Mollie wondered suspiciously. Drugs?

Before she could pursue the thought a small boy came running up to them, panting, 'Someone's coming, in a Land Rover. He's driven across the fields…'

The couple at the gate exchanged looks.

'That will be him,' the girl announced positively, and in her voice Mollie could hear elation as well as defiance.

She could now see the Land Rover as it crested the slope of the field on the opposite side of the road. It stopped a couple of yards short of the field gate. Mollie tensed as its door opened. She already knew who she was going to see getting out of it.

CHAPTER FOUR

SHE was right.

'Does *he* own this land?' she asked Sylvie darkly as she watched Alex striding towards them.

'Yes,' she acknowledged, without taking her eyes off him.

'Sylvie!'

They might have been lovers once but there was certainly nothing remotely lover-like in Alex's voice now, Mollie recognised as she heard the curt anger with which he addressed the other girl.

'I suppose I should have guessed...'

'I'm surprised you didn't,' she responded hardily, tilting her chin up at him and then tugging on the arm of her boyfriend as she drew Alex's attention to him and demanded, 'I expect you'll remember Wayne?'

There was a small pause before Alex responded quietly.

'Unfortunately, yes.'

As she watched the two men exchange a look she didn't fully understand, Mollie felt a chill of apprehension ice down her spine, and then, with a taunting smile, Wayne jerked his thumb in the direction of the wood behind them and said mockingly, 'Looks like we're going to be neighbours...'

From the way Alex's mouth hardened, Mollie wouldn't have been surprised if he had retaliated physically, but instead he turned aside and said slowly to Sylvie, 'It's taken three years to redevelop this wood. The land was cleared voluntarily by teams of local enthusiasts. This summer, for the first time, it became home to several rare species of plants. You used to feel so passionately about conservation, Sylvie, what happened to you?'

'You did. You happened to me,' she responded fiercely, but Mollie could see the tears filling her eyes and her heart went out to her.

Impulsively she stepped forward. 'They have a right to be here.'

Mollie wasn't sure who looked the more surprised, Sylvie or Alex.

'A right...what right...?' he challenged her cynically.

'The right of the common people to the land,' Mollie retaliated.

Sylvie was smiling at her, her tears banished.

'You see,' she told Alex triumphantly. 'Everyone isn't on *your* side. We're here now and we intend to stay and there's nothing you can do about it.'

'You can't stay here, Sylvie. You know—'

Instinctively he ducked as someone threw a stone at him.

'Looks like this time round might is on our side as well as right.' Wayne smirked at him as a second and third stone followed the first.

'You can't stay here,' Alex repeated, cursing under his breath as he only just managed to dodge one of the flying missiles. The group of men and women who had gathered to throw them had grown, Mollie recognised, alarm feathering along her spine as she realised that she as well as Alex was the object of their menacing looks and mutters.

'Who's going to stop us?' Sylvie crowed. 'Not you.'

'No, not me,' Alex agreed quietly. 'But this country is run by the rule of the law, Sylvie, *not* the rule of force. The law protects my rights as a land-owner, just as I, as a land-owner, protect the rights of the families and living things that inhabit the land.'

'We inhabit it now,' Sylvie told him.

'You're destroying it,' Alex retaliated coldly. 'Look around you,' he counselled her. 'Look at that sapling over there. Yes, that's the one,' he agreed as both Sylvie and Mollie instinctively followed his gaze to where it rested on the damaged sapling Mollie had noticed earlier. 'Until you arrived it was a living, breathing part of the landscape. Now it will die.'

'We have to live and breathe too,' Sylvie told him passionately.

'Indeed. But not here.'

'Then where? Where would you have us live, Alex? Some city slum neatly and tidily out of your way…out of your sight?'

Mollie saw Alex give her a calmly level look as he ignored the hail of stones and even clods of earth that were being hurled at them, and the angry chants of the growing crowd of antagonistic travellers.

'*You* have a home, Sylvie, and—'

'That isn't a home, it's a prison,' she snapped back at him, 'and you know it because you're the one—'

Mollie gasped in shock as she heard someone fire a gun. One of the men in the crowd lowered a shotgun and, grinning insolently at Alex, announced, 'Whoops, missed…this time.'

A handful of small sharp stones showered down on Mollie, thrown by a small child who stood laughing triumphantly as one of them struck her face. A much larger and potentially more lethal stone just missed Alex.

'I hope you remember to write about this,' she heard Alex telling her grittily as he grabbed hold of her arm and, before she could find the breath to protest or stop him, started to hustle her towards the Land Rover, using his body to shield her own from the battery of stones and lumps of earth that were being thrown at them.

'Let go of me. I've got my own car,' Mollie started to protest as he directed her across the road.

'You mean you *had*,' Alex told her trenchantly, and added, 'If that's it over there you won't be going very far in it now; someone's let the tyres down.'

To her dismay, Mollie saw that he was right.

Why had they damaged *her* car? *She* hadn't done them any harm. *She* wasn't the one who was antagonistic towards them.

'It's just part and parcel of their culture,' she heard Alex telling her, as though he had read her mind.

'My God, that was close,' he added feelingly as a clod of earth sailed past his head, showering pieces of soil onto them both. 'Let's get the hell out of here before they decide to turn really nasty…'

'I'm not going anywhere with you…' Mollie began to say, but he wasn't listening to her.

The Land Rover door was flung open and a harsh male voice commanded, 'Get in.'

For a second Mollie hesitated, torn between pride and relief, pausing to give a backward glance over her shoulder at the mob behind them—for it could be called no less now.

'Don't even think about it,' Alex warned her, accurately guessing what was going on in her mind. 'They won't listen to you. Half of them are high on drugs and the other half, even more dangerously, are high on the kick they get from being violent and self-righteous.'

And then, before she could say or do anything, he grabbed hold of her, virtually throwing her up into the Land Rover before slamming the door and then getting into the driver's seat and starting up the engine.

'You had no right to do that,' Mollie protested as he swiftly turned the vehicle round and started to drive away.

'Save it,' Alex told her acerbically. 'Or would you rather I turned back and threw you to the wolves?'

'They're not wolves,' she began, 'they're...they're people, human beings, with feelings...and...and rights...'

'So are those who live around here,' Alex countered.

He had a point, but it wasn't one that Mollie wanted to listen to right now. She had, after all, always been on the side of the underdog, and now that she was safely away from the mob it was easy to ignore how threatening and intimidating they had been.

'I suppose *you'd* like to have them all thrown in prison...or deported...' she accused him.

He gave a dry bark of laughter.

'Has anyone ever suggested you might be well advised to curb that over-active imagination of yours?' he demanded, and then answered his own question with a rough, 'No, I don't suppose they have.

'Listen, that mob, that crowd down there, *might* have amongst its number people who are genuinely peaceful. In fact, I'm sure it does. But it also contains a far more dangerous element. Wayne Ferris, for example—'

'Sylvie's boyfriend?' Mollie interrupted him.

'Sylvie's boyfriend, yes,' he agreed curtly.

'Ferris is known to the police as a suspected drug dealer, although they've never been able to prove anything, and that's why the situation isn't as simple as you might think. It isn't just about a homeless band of gentle travellers looking for somewhere to stay.'

'Maybe not, but would you be so concerned if it wasn't your land they were on, or if you and Sylvie hadn't once been...?'

Uncomfortably Mollie looked away from him. As a reporter it was her responsibility, her *duty*, to remain unbiased and to report on the situation fairly, but she had to admit that her sympathies really lay with the travellers.

'They just want somewhere to stay,' she told him quietly, gasping in protest as the Land Rover bumped uncomfortably over the rutted track they were on.

'Who told you that?' he challenged her cynically. 'If they just wanted "somewhere to stay", as you put it, then why aren't they applying for permission to stop at the designated site less than ten miles away at Little Barlow, where they've got proper facilities laid on? Why come here, where—'

He broke off and cursed under his breath. 'Of

course. I know who I've got to blame for that. Sylvie knows...'

He paused, and Mollie couldn't resist suggesting, 'Perhaps she has a grudge against you and she feels justified in...in...' In hurting you as much as you've obviously hurt her, she wanted to say, but something stopped her. And, of course, that 'something' had *nothing* whatsoever to do with the small sharp pain that had begun deep inside her the moment she had recognised who Sylvie's ex-lover actually was... nothing whatsoever. How could it?

They had crossed several fields now, and after driving across the last one they had moved onto a less bumpy track, leading towards a house which lay nestled in the small hollow beneath them.

'What's that?' Mollie demanded as she stared at it, determined not to let him see how impressed she was both with the house's setting and the house itself.

It was the kind of house she had dreamed of as a little girl. Palladian and lovely, elegant and timeless, set against a backdrop of rolling green English countryside, larger, perhaps, than her dream house had been...but still, despite its imposing size, retaining the air of homeliness which had taken her breath away at her first glimpse of it.

'Home,' Alex told her briefly, answering her question.

'Home...your home? You can't take me there,' she protested, but he was ignoring her as the Land Rover rattled ever closer to the house.

They drove through a brick archway and into a paved courtyard complete with tubs and urns overflowing with a profusion of flowering plants. In the silence that followed the switching off of the Land Rover's engine, Mollie could hear the drowsy, contented hum of bees. Through the open windows she could smell the scent of the flowers and feel the warmth of the sun in which the house basked, mellow and content.

In the building of this house man and nature had conspired together to create a harmonious picture of perfection, Mollie admitted reluctantly.

'It's this way,' she heard Alex telling her. Dizzily she focused on him. She had been too preoccupied with taking in the picture made by the house to register the fact that he had walked round to her door and was now holding it open for her.

Silently she allowed him to direct her towards the house, which, it was obvious, they were entering through the domestic quarters. To her surprise, along the way he paused, automatically dead-heading some of the flowers in the tubs.

The domestic quarters had quite obviously been modernised very recently, Mollie acknowledged as she was ushered into a very large and comfortable kitchen, pristinely clean apart from the papers on the large rectangular table.

'I've been working here whilst Jane is away,' Alex told her. 'Sit down. I'll put the kettle on. I want to ring the police to...'

He would put the kettle on? Where was the battalion of staff she had assumed he must need?

'What's wrong?' he asked Mollie quizzically.

'Where is everyone? You said you'd put the kettle on,' she blurted out. 'You can't live somewhere like this on your own...'

The dark eyebrows rose.

'Why not? But no, you're right. Normally speaking, I don't. But Jane, my housekeeper, has had to take time off to look after her father, who's recently had a heart attack, and the rest of the staff work nine to five and don't live in. Now, which do you prefer—tea or coffee?' he asked dutifully.

'Er...coffee, please,' Mollie heard herself responding.

Where on earth was Alex? Mollie wondered broodingly as she stared at her now empty coffee mug. Ten minutes ago he had left her, announcing that he had a couple of telephone calls to make, and he still hadn't returned.

Her curiosity getting the better of her, Mollie got up and walked towards the kitchen door, opening it and stepping into the corridor that lay beyond it.

The house was larger than she had imagined, and even more impressive, and within seconds of stepping from the corridor into what turned out to be the main entrance hallway she had fallen hopelessly under its spell, wandering awestruck from room to room.

When Alex finally caught up with her she was standing in the middle of the green drawing room, an expression of beatific pleasure illuminating her face—an expression which faded to be replaced by one of truculent distrust as she saw Alex standing watching her.

'You were gone ages...and I...I thought—'

'Yes. I'm sorry. My phone calls took longer than I had expected,' he interrupted her, generously accepting her face-saving excuse.

'The house has quite an interesting history,' he told her, coming to stand beside her and adding, 'It was originally built by *this* gentleman, whose portrait we have here.' He gestured towards the oil painting that hung above the marble fireplace.

'He built it using his wife's money—that money being the reason he married her, I regret to say. Her portrait hangs in the gallery upstairs, along with those of all the other wives. If you come this way I'll show you...'

'How fitting and how typical that your wives should be banished upstairs,' Mollie couldn't resist commenting loftily as she followed him back to the hallway and its twin staircases.

'*I* don't happen to have a wife,' Alex corrected her. 'If I did, her place—'

'Her *place*...?' Mollie interrupted him bitingly.

'Her place,' he continued placidly, 'would be at my side.'

He paused and looked at her as he waited for her to precede him up the stairs.

'As mine would be at hers...'

Unable to stop herself, Mollie muttered under her breath, 'Tell that to Sylvie.' She turned away as she did so, but he had obviously heard her. He caught hold of her arm as he demanded, 'Why... what does it have to do with Sylvie?'

Heavens, but he was hard—and cold. He was a man in his thirties; Sylvie could only have been a young teenager when she had... when he had...

'She was your lover until... until you threw her out,' Mollie reminded him.

She could see from the shock on his face that he

had not expected her to challenge him so directly, but when he threw back his head and started to laugh it was *her* turn to be shocked.

'How can you?' she stormed at him. 'She was a girl...a child, practically...and you...'

'Hang on a minute.' He had stopped laughing now, his eyes narrowing as he told her, 'Sylvie and I have not nor ever could be lovers, and why on earth you should think we might...'

'Sylvie said she lived with you for four years,' Mollie told him trenchantly.

'So she did,' he agreed instantly. 'But as my step-sister, not my lover. Her mother was my father's second wife. Sylvie is her daughter by her first husband.'

They had reached the top of the stairs now, and Mollie could feel the hot colour flooding her face as she took in what he had just said.

Abruptly she sat down on the pale duck-egg-blue satin-covered *fauteuil* chair behind her.

'Sylvie is your stepsister?'

'Unfortunately, yes.'

Unfortunately. Mollie's head snapped up, her eyes flashing.

'If she's your stepsister, then why is she...?'

'Living rough with a drug dealer?' he finished grimly for her. 'You tell me, because *she* certainly won't. She dropped out of university ostensibly because she could no longer allow herself to live the kind of privileged, useless life she had hitherto apparently quite happily enjoyed—until Wayne showed her the shallow error of her ways. Sylvie has, unfortunately, always been a trifle immature—the result of

an over-protective mother. It was perhaps inevitable
that she would kick over the traces.'

'But you'd rather it was not with Wayne,' Mollie
guessed.

'Not with Wayne,' Alex agreed sombrely. 'I don't
think she realises quite what she's got herself into.
Despite everything I've tried to tell her she refuses to
accept what Wayne really is.'

'What you *believe* he really is.' Mollie felt obliged
to correct him. 'You said yourself that the police had
been unable to prove that he was dealing drugs.'

'Sylvie met Wayne at a rave party. One of the boys
who attended it—a boy, who was the same age as
Sylvie—died after taking Ecstasy at the rave. The police are pretty sure the drug was supplied by Wayne.'

Mollie bit her lip. There was nothing she could say.
She hadn't liked Wayne herself, but that didn't mean
that Alex was right about him. Give a dog a bad name,
et cetera...

'The portrait gallery is along here,' Alex told her,
touching her arm lightly to guide her across the land-
ing.

'This is the older part of the house,' he explained
as Mollie gazed at the corridor's vaulted and intri-
cately plastered ceiling. 'The Palladian façade was
built onto what was left of the original house, which
had been badly damaged in a fire.

'This gallery dates back to Queen Elizabeth the
First's reign, as does the Queen's bedroom which
leads off it—so named because supposedly Elizabeth
herself slept there.'

'The *Queen's* bedroom?' Mollie questioned, in-
trigued.

'Yes. It's here,' Alex told her, going to open a pair of doors several feet away.

Mollie gasped in delight as she stepped into the room.

Long years ago, as an idealistic young teenager, her imagination fired by the many historical books she had read, she had fantasised about making love in just such a room—carried there by her ardent lover and wooed sensuously and blissfully in just such a deliciously romantic four-poster bed.

'What is it? What's wrong?' Alex asked her softly, watching her as she stood silently studying the room with wondering eyes, looking, he decided, not unlike a small child faced with the awesome delights of an unexpected Christmas tree, complete with brightly wrapped presents.

'It's…it's this room,' Mollie told him huskily. 'It's just…it's perfect.'

'Perfect for what?' he asked her quizzically, smiling at her, his smile dying away as he saw the self-conscious tide of colour flushing her skin.

'It…it reminds me of a silly teenage fantasy I used to have,' Mollie admitted reluctantly, guessing that he would press her until she made some response and unable to come up with a suitable fib.

She turned hastily towards the door, suddenly anxious to escape the room and the provocative memories it was still stirring—along with its even more provocative owner. For no good reason that she could think of she was suddenly remembering how she had felt when he had kissed her, how *he* had felt, how she had responded to him, been aroused by him…how she was in danger of being aroused by him right now.

But he didn't seem anything like as anxious to leave the bedroom as she was, standing leaning calmly against the closed door and blocking her exit as he questioned, 'You mean you used to imagine you were Queen Elizabeth?'

Mollie gave him an exasperated look.

'No. Of course not,' she told him scornfully. 'It wasn't *that* kind of fantasy at all.'

'No? Then what kind of fantasy was it?'

A dangerous tension seemed to have crept into the room, infiltrating the very air she was breathing, Mollie recognised, increasing her heartbeat and affecting every one of her five senses, making her feel, making her *want*...

Hastily, she glanced away from the bed, with its heavy damask drapes and its inviting soft white bed-linen, wishing she couldn't remember *quite* so vividly how she had lain on her own narrow single bed, heatedly fantasising about lying in the cool privacy of just such a bed, naked with her lover, as he stroked her and kissed her, the warm scents of a summer's evening drifting in through the open window whilst on the fire the logs he had lit to warm her nakedness burned to ash, her warmth now provided by the heat of their mutual passion and her lover's vigorously ardent body...

It appalled her how easy it was for her to transfer those long-ago images to the present, and to the bed in front of her. Only now they had adult forms and faces, and the lover who was holding her, touching her, was...

Trembling from head to foot, she turned away from Alex.

In the hearth a fire had been laid with logs ready to be lit; the leaded windows were open to the now fading light. Two large pewter candelabra stood on the oak chest beneath the window. How often in her secret fantasy had she visualised herself watching in quivering anticipation as her lover slowly extinguished the flames of just such a light before equally slowly and sensuously undressing her, kissing every inch of her skin as he did so, stroking her body, teasing it, drawing from it a response that had made her cry out in a tormented mixture of longing and excitement as she lay on her solitary virgin bed?

'What kind of fantasy?' Alex repeated softly.

Dry-mouthed, Mollie looked at him. Something in his eyes, in the way he was watching her, mesmerised her, bewitched her almost. She could feel the fierce, heavy thud of her own heartbeat shaking her body with each portentous blow.

That's none of your business, she had been about to say, but instead, almost as though the words were being conjured from her by some magical power she was unable to resist, she heard herself saying in a low, sensuously slow voice, 'The kind that all teenage girls have, about…about the man they want to be their lover.

'I read historical novels, so my lover…' She paused, her expression more revealing and illuminating than she knew as she looked from him to the four-poster bed and then back again. 'I imagined that we would make love in a room like this…a bed like that,' she told him, nodding in the direction of the bed.

'It would be dark, with candles lit, and the fire— he would light it to keep us warm, even though… We would drink red wine, full-bodied and rich, and it would spill down onto my gown, my skin...'

Dreamily Mollie closed her eyes, almost forgetting where she was and who she was with as she let herself become mesmerised by the drowsy, hypnotic sound of her own voice and the power of the sensual memories she had unleashed.

'We would undress each other slowly, kissing and touching...' A sensual shiver ran through Mollie's body.

Then, her fantasising had not gone much further than mere touching and kissing. Now...

Helplessly her gaze was dragged back to the bed, and then to the man still leaning against the door. Undressed he would present a far more muscular and physically male lover than the one who had inhabited her fantasies. A fully adult man, not a boy. Just as she was a fully adult woman. Her body quivered again as sensual heat flooded her.

'I...I must go,' she told Alex in a husky voice. 'My article...'

'Can wait. The *Gazette* doesn't come out for another three days,' Alex reminded her.

'I want to go back, to interview the travellers, hear their individual stories...'

'You can't. The police intend to cordon off the whole area,' Alex told her softly.

'What...what are you doing...?' Mollie asked him uncertainly as he suddenly turned and locked the bedroom door, pocketing the iron key and then walking across the room towards the fire, answering her as he knelt down to strike a match to light it.

'As a youth *I* had a similar fantasy. Only mine fea-

tured a warm, sensual, loving, golden-eyed girl with
curls that lay tousled on the pillow in the aftermath
of our loving and eyes that could be as fiery as those
of a tigress and as soft as those of a kitten.'

He was lighting the candles in the candelabra now.
Bemused, Mollie watched as they threw dancing
shadows across the room.

'My lover was as slender and graceful as a nymph,
silken-skinned and honey-sweet, her loving generous
and so pleasurable that... How was yours?' he asked
her softly as he put down the candelabra and closed
the distance between them.

It must be the scent of the candles and the logs that
was making her head swim, Mollie decided dizzily as
his arms closed around her and she let them.

'Mine was...' she began. 'Mine was...'

She discovered she was mumbling the words
against his lips, lips that were gently and oh, so deliciously teasing and caressing hers, softly prising
them apart so that his tongue could dart between
them, alternately giving and taking. She could feel
what he was doing to her, right down to her toes.

'This isn't a fantasy,' she protested.

'No, it isn't,' she heard him agree as he picked her
up and carried her towards the bed.

CHAPTER FIVE

'WE SHOULDN'T be doing this...'

Why did her voice sound so slurred, so uncertain, so full of unconscious and unadmitted pleading for him to contradict her? Mollie wondered despairingly as she struggled to resist the temptation to give in to the sensations storming her body.

The bed felt every bit as soft as she'd imagined. The sheets smelled of lavender, their scent mingling with that of the logs and the roses beneath the window, but more alluring and sensual by far was the scent of Alex's body. And if she was so aware, so responsive to it, to *him* now, when he was still fully dressed, how was she going to feel when...once...?

'Tell me to stop and I will,' she heard him responding huskily. 'God, but I want you,' he added in a much stronger and more raw voice, the expression in his eyes as she lifted her head to look at him confirming the intensity of his need.

'This is crazy,' Mollie protested weakly.

'Madness,' he agreed, before bending his head to kiss the exposed curve of her throat just where it met her shoulder.

Mollie closed her eyes, her whole body convulsed by deep shudders of physical pleasure. If he could affect her like that, just by kissing her skin there, then how...?

The look she gave him, her eyes dazed and smoky, made his fingers tremble as he started to undress her.

Mutely Mollie watched him as he removed her top, exposing her breasts. Very gently he pressed her back against the piled-up white pillows, leaning over to slide his fingers into her hair, letting it slip through them whilst he studied her eyes and then her mouth.

Mollie could feel the soft fabric of his shirt just grazing the tips of her breasts, the sensation impossibly, agonisingly erotic. He was kneeling on the bed, straddling her, his torso still semi-clothed, his whole concentration focused on her face, her hair, her eyes, her mouth.

With a soft moan Mollie closed her eyes again, her tongue-tip moistening her parted lips. She felt the shudder that jolted through him as he bent his head to kiss her open mouth.

'Oh, God, God,' she heard him groan as he cupped her face and held her prisoner beneath the fierce passion of his kiss, his tongue thrusting hungrily into her mouth, sensuously demanding that she give every bit of herself to him, that she yield up every last bit of her female self to his maleness.

Helplessly, Mollie responded to the overwhelming intensity of his passion, recognising it as a tribute to and an acknowledgement of the irresistible force of her womanhood.

He was *her* man. Her *mate*, her fantasy and her destiny. To deny him, to deny herself would be a rejection of her deepest self. Their coming together was fate, preordained, impossible to deny.

The heat coming off his body burned the air that touched her naked breasts, making them ache hotly for his touch, his mouth. Instinctively, she took his hand and guided it to one of them, trembling as she felt his whole body shudder in response to the feel of her soft naked flesh.

He was kissing her eyes, her cheeks, her throat, whilst slowly lifting his body away from hers.

Semi-drugged with arousal, Mollie opened her eyes and watched him as he slowly studied her naked breasts. Very gently he reached out and teased one of her tousled curls down over her skin.

'You've the most wonderful hair,' he told her rawly. 'It makes me want to...'

Mollie could feel and see her reaction to the way his words aroused her showing in her tightly swollen breasts and pouting nipples. And she knew that he could see it as well. She watched his expression change as he looked from her eyes to her breasts. Very slowly he reached out and touched them, stroking their soft skin with deliciously erotic fingertips, curling them into the hard warmth of his palms and then circling her flushed and wanton nipples with his thumbs.

Mollie closed her eyes and moaned softly beneath her breath, her whole body trembling.

'Do you like that...? Does it feel good?'

Helplessly she nodded.

Alex's hands left her breasts and he reached for the fastening on her jeans.

Momentarily Mollie tensed.

'I want to see all of you,' Alex told her softly. 'See, touch, know and taste.'

An explosion of sensation ripped through her, making her shiver and ache.

Outside dusk had fallen; beyond the bed the candelabra lit the room along with the fire, clothing it in soft, warm light. The same light that now clothed her bare skin, Mollie recognised as she lay proudly naked beneath the smouldering burn of Alex's silent scrutiny.

She could see the aroused colour slowly burning up under his skin, darkening his face, tautening his jawline, and it gave her a sharp thrill of pleasure to know how much he wanted her. He reached out and cupped her feet in his hands, caressing them.

Mollie felt as though she might melt. The sensation of his strong fingers massaging her feet was one that sent her delirious with pleasure, her whole body lapped in molten, golden, blissful, sensual heat. She could feel herself turning boneless, liquid, positively ready to purr with female delight.

'No. Stop…' she commanded him, when his hands started to move up over her ankles, circling their narrowness.

'I want you to take off your clothes,' she told him when he looked questioningly at her. '*I* want to see *you*.'

That had never been part of her fantasy, but that didn't matter now. Urgently, instantly she wanted— no, *needed* to see him, to see if his body could possibly be as totally physically male as the image she was conjuring up in her mind's eye.

He undressed quickly and unselfconsciously, whilst she held her breath a little nervously and watched him. By the time he had finished she felt almost giddily light-headed and dizzy, and not, she admitted, because she was holding her breath.

Physically he was...he was... Tentatively she reached out to touch the dark hair on his body, wondering if it could possibly be as soft and inviting as it looked.

It was... Mollie gave a small blissful sigh and closed her eyes, opening them again very quickly as she heard a low, raw moan.

'Don't do that to me unless you want...' he began warningly.

'Unless I want what?' Mollie suddenly felt brave enough to ask provocatively, but he wasn't listening to her.

As she moved, the light from the candles illuminated the soft rose-tipped curves of her breasts. Swiftly, as though unable to resist the temptation, he bent his head and, cupping both her breasts in his hands, began to caress first one and then the other with the warm, wet lap of his tongue. Mollie shivered in hot pleasure, throwing back her head and arching her body as she mutely invited him, unable to stop herself from showing him how much she was enjoying his tongue against her.

Very deliberately, Alex ran his tongue-tip round and then over her nipple, causing her to cry out in sharp excitement. She could feel her stomach muscles tensing against the intensity of the emotions that were filling her as Alex looked down at her body. She could see his own arousal, and she had to control an unexpected urge to reach out and touch him, to touch *it*, to see if he felt as fascinating, strong and powerful as he looked...

The very thought of how he would feel inside her made her breasts, her whole body start to throb and ache, and as though he too was affected by her thoughts, her desire, he gave a low, husky growl deep in his throat. He smoothed his hands over her thighs and before she could stop him started to cover her midriff and then her belly with the same urgent and moist lapping of his tongue with which he had earlier caressed her breasts.

It was more than Mollie was able to withstand. She could hear herself protesting that he mustn't, that he must stop, that she didn't want... Her words became a mixed jumble of breathless sounds of incoherent delight as he circled her navel with his tongue.

'This fantasy lover of yours—did he do this?' she heard him asking her throatily.

'No...no, he didn't,' Mollie managed to whisper back.

'And this...did he do this?' he demanded taking her by surprise as he took hold of her and rolled her on top of his own now supine body, kissing her lingeringly on the mouth for several bliss-filled minutes before moulding her against his body as though he couldn't get her close enough to him, and moving his mouth from her lips to her breast.

'Oh-h-h... Oh-h-h...'

Mollie heard herself moan and knew that the sound was only a small echo of the intense pleasure she was feeling as his mouth at first very gently and then, as his own needs took hold of him hungrily, almost savagely suckled on her breast. Instinctively reaching out to him, she had no idea that the increased pressure of his mouth on her body and its heated demand was in direct reaction to the aroused raking of her nails against his skin.

She could feel the hard heat of his body against hers, inciting the deep ache that was pulsing inside her as his hands slid down over her body, cupping her buttocks, caressing the smooth, soft peachiness of her feminine shape.

He lifted his mouth from her breast and whispered softly to her, 'God, you feel good—hot and sweet and all woman.'

As she eased her body slightly away from his to look at him, his hand filled the space between them, stroking down over her belly and moving lower.

Mollie trembled as his fingers stroked her sex, exploring its moist readiness for his possession. The gentleness with which he was touching her made her tremble eagerly, her body so exquisitely sensitive that she had to hold her breath.

'There. Do you like me touching you there?' he demanded huskily as he saw the way she trembled.

Over and over again his fingers stroked against the most sensitive part of her, tantalising, teasing, until she felt she could bear it no longer, her fingers curling round his wrist as she tried to push his hand away. She was breathing hard, panting almost, her bare skin bathed in a film of sensual mist. She could smell his own correspondingly aroused male heat, see it in the slick, damped-down wetness of his body hair.

'Do you want to stay there, be on top?' he asked her softly.

Hot-cheeked, Mollie nodded.

How had he known…guessed that was what she wanted…needed? A more adult fantasy than her other one, perhaps, but still so far, in real life, merely nothing more than that—a fantasy.

'Come on, then,' he urged her, watching, guiding her as she positioned herself over him, holding her, helping her.

Mollie closed her eyes as she eased her body down against his and then opened them again, shuddering in silent awed pleasure as her body opened to his penetration, holding him still, just within herself, as she savoured the sensation of actually feeling him, experiencing him, his heat, his power and strength, and the hot liquid pleasure it caused within her.

Lost in the sensuality of the pleasure she was experiencing, it was several seconds before she realised that the sound she could hear was the tortured grinding of his teeth.

'Have you any idea just what you're doing to me?' he demanded thickly as she made a soft moan of pleasure and allowed him to move deeper within her, and then deeper again, and again and again. She was no longer the one in control of what was happening between them, Mollie recognised, even if officially she was the one 'on top'.

Neither of them was in control; their bodies, their needs, their desires had taken that control away from them as Alex grasped her hips and tried to control the fierce, hungry thrusting of his body within hers.

But she didn't need him to control it. She *wanted* to feel him like this, to know him like this—to feel and know the fierce, urgent, thrusting hunger of him wanting her, and her own response to that wanting as her body gloried in its feminine power over him, gloried in it and then forgot it as her own desire overwhelmed her.

Mollie cried out to him in delirious ecstasy as her

body tightened itself around him before exploding in a starburst of pleasure-loaded contractions that seemed to reach out from the centre of her body and made her gasp his name and cling helplessly to him whilst she shuddered uncontrollably in his arms.

She could feel his release as her own died away, would have known of it even without the harsh cry of completion he gave. Sleepy and satiated, Mollie lay in his arms as he kissed her and stroked her skin, and thought, before sleep claimed her, that it was an odd coincidence that they should have shared the same fantasy.

Several hours later, when she eventually woke up, she wondered at first where on earth she was, and then she saw Alex standing beside the fire, feeding it with fresh logs. He turned round and looked at her even though she hadn't made a sound to betray the fact that she was awake, and as he did so she saw the long dark scratches on his arms and back.

Hot colour suffused her skin. Had *she* done that?

The candelabra had been filled with fresh candles and on the chest beside them stood an open bottle of red wine and some crusty bread and pâté.

'I thought you might be hungry,' Alex told her, gesturing towards the bread, and Mollie blushed even harder as she remembered just why he might think that.

She found it hard to believe what she had done. What she had *done*, maybe, but not how she had felt, she acknowledged as he straightened up and walked towards her, and her body, her senses reminded her of just what she had felt in his arms. Just what she was beginning to feel again right now.

Nervously she licked her suddenly too dry lips. Not again. She couldn't; they couldn't.

Alex was pouring them both a glass of wine. He came over to the bed and handed one of them to Mollie. Her hand was trembling so much that she spilled some of it, the dark red droplets splashing down onto his hand and from his hand onto her naked body.

Very deliberately he bent his head and licked the spilled wine, first from his own wrist and then, without taking his eyes off her, from her arm. The shudder that ran through her was so deep and intense that she could feel it at the very core of her being, so intense that a few more droplets of wine fell from the base of the glass onto her naked thigh.

Wordlessly Mollie watched Alex silently take the glass from her and put down his own before dipping his finger in the wine puddled on her thigh and lifting it to his mouth.

'Do you know what I feel like doing?' He asked her softly, still watching her. 'Right now I would like to take that bottle of wine and pour the whole lot slowly, very slowly, all over you and then, even more slowly, and very, very thoroughly, drink it off your skin.

'Drink you,' he told her hoarsely, his glance dipping from her face to the dark juncture of her thighs and her sex.

Mollie felt the heat already pulsing inside her turning into an agonised, sharply racking ache, an explosion of need so intense and unexpected that she was moving towards him before she even knew what she was doing.

And it wasn't just *his* mouth that caressed and enjoyed *her* sex, that gave the gift of sensual oral pleasure and caused its recipient to cry out in mortal ecstasy at such a heavenly gift.

It wasn't just *he* who drank the rich, mellow wine from *her* body. This time they made love more slowly and languorously, his long, slow strokes within her body making her moan softly in sensual pleasure.

This time they finished together, in a mutual explosive need that racked both their bodies and left them breathless and trembling as they wrapped their arms around one another.

This time before she fell asleep Mollie knew that she was beginning to feel afraid. What was happening between them…to her…this wasn't just lust…desire. This was… This was something dangerous and unplanned—something she hadn't wanted to have in her life, with someone she certainly didn't want to have in her life.

Desperately she closed her eyes, pushing away the truth, trying to comfort the panic as she recognised just what it was she was trying so hard to deny she could feel.

CHAPTER SIX

At six o'clock on a summer morning the town of Fordcaster was thankfully empty, so that Mollie was able to park Alex's purloined Land Rover outside her house and scuttle indoors without anyone having seen her.

It had been a piece of good fortune that Alex had left the keys in the Land Rover, so that after she had woken up and sneaked downstairs, leaving him sleeping, she had been able to drive away without having to make any explanations.

Her body still ached from the intensity of their lovemaking and she knew that the memory of the pleasure they had shared would be inscribed on her heart for ever. But even more sharply intense was the sense of foreboding and apprehension with which she had woken this morning, the knowledge of how frighteningly easy it would be for her to want, to *need* far more from Alex than the sensuously thrilling intimacy they had shared last night.

In her heart of hearts she knew that it was perhaps already too late, that she was already emotionally drawn to him, emotionally dangerously vulnerable to him.

She had left him a note, scribbling it down on a page from her notebook, telling him that last night was something she believed they would both be better off forgetting.

Forgetting. Small chance of her being able to do that, she acknowledged, no matter how resolutely she might try to push it to the back of her mind.

She scrubbed vigorously at the sink she was cleaning, her face growing hot as she remembered certain events of the night.

She must have been mad to tell him about her silly teenage fantasy like that. Why on earth *had* she? It was totally unlike her to be so...so...forthcoming, especially about something so essentially private. Why, in any other woman she might almost have been tempted to put such behaviour down to an inherent desire to provoke exactly the reaction her own disclosures had elicited from Alex...

Her body tensed. No, she assured herself fiercely. She had not deliberately provoked and teased Alex into making love to her. Not consciously, perhaps, her stern inner critic agreed.

No buts, she told herself sternly; it was over, finished. Nothing had actually ever been started; last night had been a mistake, totally, utterly and completely, and it certainly wasn't one she intended to repeat. Ever...

It was now almost eight. When she got to work she wanted to write up her copy for the piece Bob wanted on the travellers.

She had turned on the radio and the television when she had come in, hoping to catch up with any news items regarding their arrival, but so far there hadn't been any.

She had left Alex a second note, informing him that she was borrowing the Land Rover and telling him that she would leave the key at the newspaper's offices for him to collect, but just for a second, as she opened her front door on her way to work and saw a police car cruising slowly down the street, she cringed, wondering if Alex could possibly have deliberately ignored her note and reported the vehicle as stolen. But it was only for a second.

Without being able to analyse why, somehow she knew instinctively that was just not the kind of thing he would do. Although just because he had been such a wonderful lover that did not mean... Hastily she pushed such thoughts to the back of her mind. *That* had been a mistake and should never have happened, would never happen again.

As she walked through the town she noticed that a couple of shop windows had been boarded up. The owner of one was still sweeping up the glass outside one of them.

'What happened?' Mollie asked him sympathetically.

'It was those travellers—a whole bunch of them. They shouldn't be here. Something's going to have to be done—lazy good-for-nothings, never done a proper day's work in their lives, most of them...'

Mollie had to stop herself from arguing with him and trying to defend the travellers, and heroically she managed to do so. They were, after all, a group of people comprised of individuals, just as the townspeople were also individuals, but she could see that the shopkeeper was not in the right frame of mind to listen to any kind of defence of them.

Once she reached the newspaper's offices she found her colleagues in very much the same frame of mind as the shopkeeper.

'And the little so-and-so had the cheek to tell me that I owed him two pounds,' one of them was saying when Mollie walked in through the door.

'First he jumps out at me at the traffic lights and nearly gives me a heart attack, and then, when I get out of the car, he claims that he wasn't going to try to snatch my jacket from the passenger seat at all and that he was only going to wash the car windows...'

'Perhaps he was,' Mollie suggested unwisely.

'Without any water or a cloth?' the other man sneered. 'Something's going to have to be done,' he finished, unwittingly repeating the shopkeeper's words from earlier.

'Something will be done,' Bob Fleury announced firmly, walking into the main office on the tail of this comment. 'This news blackout that's been imposed should at least prevent any more travellers from being tempted to join them. The police have got the area cordoned off now, which hopefully should contain them and prevent any more incidents in town and give us time for a proper strategy to be worked out...'

'Legally—' Mollie began, but was overruled as someone else chimed in angrily.

'The only strategy that lot will understand is one that involves being told that they've got to move on. If you want my opinion, what Alex should have done was got together a decent-sized group of men and gone down there and sent them on their way before they had time to get themselves so nicely settled...'

'Used force and violence against them, you mean?' Mollie demanded, aghast.

'Have you got a better idea?' he asked her acidly.

'You were down there yesterday, weren't you? Have you seen what they're doing to that wood?'

Mollie bit her lip. She had to admit that the desecration of such a beautiful spot was something she found hard to excuse.

'All they want is to be left in peace to live their own lifestyle—' she began, but the other man laughed bitterly.

'Come off it,' he told her. 'That's the last thing they want. What they want is to attract as much media interest and cause as much mayhem as they can. They're confrontation junkies; they love having all the attention, causing a lot of problems. If they didn't, they wouldn't have stopped here. They'd have gone straight on to Little Barlow...'

'I've heard that Sylvie, Alex's stepsister, is with them,' one of the reporters intervened.

Both men looked at Mollie.

'Well, if she is, then that explains a lot,' Lucy, Bob's secretary, put in. 'She adored Alex when their parents first got married. I can remember how she used to follow him everywhere. But her mother was one of those very possessive women, though at the same time never seemed to have an awful lot of time for Sylvie. Sylvie was at boarding-school when her mother married Alex's father, and then she went straight from there to university.

'I can remember at the time that Alex wanted her to be encouraged to take a year out. He thought it would do her good, give her a bit of independence, but her mother had other ideas. I believe she wanted to send her to some Swiss finishing school type of place, but Sylvie refused to go. I don't think it really came as any surprise to Alex when she finally rebelled and dropped out of university...'

'Has she got some kind of grudge against Alex?' the other reporter asked her bluntly. 'Do you think that that's why they ventured up this way, chose to turn up here...?'

'I'm not sure about a grudge,' Carol, Bob's advertising manager answered carefully. 'Certainly she would have no reason to have one. As Lucy said before, she adored Alex and used to follow him everywhere when she was home from school. In fact, there was a rumour at the time of his father's death, and after his stepmother's decision to live in London, that Sylvie begged both Alex and her mother to be allowed to live here with him.

'If she ought to have a grudge against anyone I should have thought it would be her mother, although teenage girls are notorious for the intensity of their emotions—as I know to my cost, being the mother of three of them,' she added with a wry smile.

Silently, Mollie absorbed her comments. They threw an illuminating beam of light on what little she had known of Alex's relationship with Sylvie. Despite what the older woman had said, Mollie guessed from the comments which Sylvie had made that the younger girl *did* perhaps feel that Alex had let her down at some stage in their relationship by not agreeing to have her to live with him.

It brought up an interesting angle to the travellers' arrival in the area, and one that, as a journalist, Mollie knew could provide an extremely newsworthy 'human element' to the whole story. However, she doubted that Alex himself was likely to prove very informative on the subject, even if she could bring herself to break the promise she had made herself and seek him out to cross-question him. Sylvie, though, might be more than willing to discuss their relationship.

Absently, Mollie nibbled on one of the home-made biscuits Carol had brought in to distribute around the office for elevenses.

'I used to make them for the girls,' she had sighed as she'd offered Mollie one. 'But now Karen's at university, Mel's refusing to eat anything that isn't "low fat", and Samantha's decided she's a strict vegetarian.

'I still keep baking them, though, and since my waistline doesn't need any encouragement to expand—it can do that very nicely on its own these days, thank you very much—I thought I might as well bring them into work.'

'They're delicious,' Mollie had told her, and had meant it.

Now, as the two men drifted away and Carol offered her a second one, she shook her head.

'You look tired. I suppose all the fuss in town last night kept you awake,' Carol suggested sympathetically.

'Not really. I have to admit I didn't hear it,' Mollie told her truthfully, dipping her head slightly so that the other woman wouldn't see the tell-tale blush burning her face.

'No? Well, you were lucky. According to what I've heard in the newsagent's this morning, the police were on the verge of having to call in riot reinforcements when luckily they managed to break things up. I think we're going to be in for one or two very nasty situations developing if something isn't done to sort things out soon.'

'I suppose by sorting things out you mean move the travellers on?' Mollie countered challengingly.

Carol gave her a mild look.

'Well, that's certainly the current general consensus of opinion locally.'

'Hasn't it occurred to anyone living here that if they treated the travellers with a bit of kindness and warmth…? They are, after all, human beings; we are all part of the same race. All they want is somewhere to settle themselves for the winter. Somewhere to live with their children…'

Carol smiled and shook her head, and then said gently to Mollie when she saw her defensively angry expression, 'I'm sorry, it's just that you remind me so much of Karen, my eldest daughter. She's like you, very idealistic, and she feels very strongly about things. I'm sure you're right when you say that the majority of the travellers do simply want to live peaceably,' she told Mollie palliatively, 'but it has to be said that there is an element amongst them who seem to want no such thing. I can well understand why local opinion is that the travellers should be moved on…'

'Against their will and by force?' Mollie asked her unhappily.

'Well, that wouldn't be my choice,' Carol acknowledged, 'but some of the farmers are bound to see the travellers as a threat to their own livelihood. The odd vagrant sleeping rough in the barn is one thing; such a wholesale invasion of their territory by a virtual army of people who don't share their own respect for the countryside is quite another.'

'The land belongs to...Alex,' Mollie pointed out.

'Yes, that is a very definite plus point,' Carol said, her comment catching Mollie slightly off guard.

'Why should the fact that *he* owns it be an advantage?' she asked her frowningly, her frown deepening as she guessed. 'I suppose you mean that he's wealthy enough to be able to hire people to move the travellers off his land...'

Carol stared at her, openly astonished.

'Alex would never do anything like that,' she told Mollie very firmly and positively. 'He's far too...too much of a humanist for anything like that. No, what I actually meant was that since the wood belongs to Alex he might be able to damp down any of the local hotheads who might otherwise have decided to take matters into their own hands. Knowing Alex, he's far more likely to try to help the travellers than to hinder them.

'Every summer he has a huge group of deprived inner-city kids out here to stay at Otel Place. Heaven knows what it must cost him, because he has to bring in extra staff to look after them. Have you seen the house yet? If you get the opportunity to do so, you must. It really is the most beautiful place, and, large though it is, it's easy to visualise it being a real home.

'When Alex's father died it was touch-and-go for a while as to whether or not the house would have to be closed. It must cost a fortune to run, even though the only live-in staff Alex has now are Jane, his housekeeper, and Ranulf Carrington, his estate manager, and even he doesn't strictly live in, since he actually lives in the gatehouse by the main entrance.

'Have you met Ran yet, by the way? He's something of a dark horse. Karen, my eldest, had rather a crush on him when he first moved into the area.'

'No...no, I haven't,' Mollie responded.

The more she heard about Alex, the more she... The more she what? Wished that people wouldn't paint such a glowing picture of him...? Wanted to hear *something* about him that would enable her to...to what? To stop thinking about him...to stop wanting him...to stop being tempted to fall in love with him?

How ridiculous. Of course she wasn't falling in love with him. She didn't feel *anything* for him, she insisted to herself. But of course she knew she was lying. There was no way she would ever have allowed what had happened between them last night to take place if she had genuinely felt nothing for him. But last night was something she didn't want to think about...wasn't *going* to think about, she told herself firmly.

Mollie frowned as she walked into the bread shop and heard the raised angry voice of the owner.

'I've already told you. You're not getting served here,' he was telling the thin young woman standing at the counter. 'You lot have already caused enough trouble.'

A dark, embarrassed flush was staining the girl's face as she started to turn away from the counter, and the curious and mostly disapproving looks of the other customers.

'Keep your bloody bread, then,' Mollie heard her mutter savagely as she stormed out of the shop. 'All I wanted was a bloody loaf...'

Acting instinctively, Mollie picked up a couple of loaves and handed the waiting assistant the money, quickly running out into the street after the girl, hurrying to catch her up.

Mollie thought she recognised her as one of the angry mob who had been hurling stones and sods at them the previous day, but that didn't matter. It was no wonder that the travellers felt persecuted and angrily defensive if they were constantly treated as she had just been.

'Wait,' she called breathlessly to her as she caught up with her. 'Here's a loaf if you want it...' Warily the girl stared at her.

'Take it,' Mollie offered, smiling at her. 'It's wholemeal. I wasn't sure...'

'Wholemeal's fine,' the girl acknowledged, taking the loaf from Mollie. 'The kids don't like it but I make them eat it. It's better for them and besides, when it's covered in baked beans they don't really notice.

'Stupid old sod,' she added, nodding in the direction of the bread shop. 'Anyone would think I'd wanted to nick his bloody bread instead of pay for it. Next time I'll buy it from the supermarket. They aren't so fussy. You'd think he'd be glad of the extra money. I mean, it's hardly stockbroker belt, is it?' she said to Mollie disparagingly, gesturing in the general direction of the town centre.

'You're the reporter, aren't you?' she went on. 'Saw you at the site yesterday. The site...' She grimaced. 'Some place that is—course, if Wayne will leave it to that bloody toffee-nosed girlfriend of his to pick a place. What does she know about what's needed?

'I suppose all she could think about was how pretty the lake was. Never thought about what it would be like for the rest of us, trying to keep the kids away from the water, getting the vans bogged down in the mud, and all those damned trees... Still, the ones we've cut down will help keep the camp fires burning,' she added, oblivious to Mollie's instinctive wince.

Alex had said that he was trying to get the woodland area listed as a conservation area and it hurt Mollie to think of the destruction of those newly planted living, growing saplings.

'If you ask me,' the girl continued, sniffing, 'we'd have been much better off at Little Barlow. They've got proper facilities there, and a pub in the village that has a great karaoke night. It's a proper lively place, where the locals make you welcome. Not like round here.' She sniffed again and then handed Mollie the money for the loaf.

'I've got to go,' she told Mollie. 'Wayne's picking me up. He had some business to do...'

Mollie frowned.

'What kind of business?' she asked, but the girl shook her head.

'Wayne's business is his business, and he doesn't like other people sticking their noses into it,' she told her pointedly, adding meaningfully, 'Got a nasty temper, Wayne has.'

'Have you known him long?' Mollie asked her

semi-casually, her frown deepening as she saw an obviously expensive BMW pull to a halt at the other end of the street. The other girl had seen it too.

'Look, there's Wayne,' she told Mollie urgently. 'I've got to go. He doesn't like being kept waiting—for anything,' she added. 'As prissy little Miss Posh is going to discover before very much longer. If she thinks that by coming on like a virgin and keeping him out of her bed she's going to make a big impression on him, she couldn't be more wrong. Wayne can get a girl to warm his bed any time he wants...'

Mollie was still frowning as she watched the other girl hurrying down the road to where Wayne was now leaning against the open door of the BMW, smoking a cigarette.

As they drove past her several minutes later, Mollie couldn't help noticing that the BMW was a brand-new model. All the other vehicles she had seen in the convoy the previous day had been old and often decrepit. Wayne must have a very good source of income if he could afford to buy and run a car like that. Reluctantly she remembered what Alex had said about the police suspecting that he was involved with drugs.

Alex's Land Rover was still parked outside her house when she returned from work. Her heart skipped a beat as she saw it but she refused to give in to the unwanted tingle of sensation that ran down her spine or the emotions which accompanied it.

All day she had been on edge, just in case he ignored her note and tried to get in touch with her either by telephone or in person, panicking about what she would do, what she would say, how she might feel if he tried to persuade her to change her mind.

What was she panicking *for*? she asked herself grimly as she unlocked the front door and bent down to pick up her mail. After all, he had said nothing to her to intimate that he *wanted* to have a formal relationship with her or make a commitment to her. He could simply have been using her and would no doubt be amused by her panic since the last thing he probably intended to do was get in touch with her. In fact, so far as he was concerned, she had probably done him a favour by leaving him that note.

Mollie frowned as she put down her post and her handbag and walked into the kitchen. Why should what she was thinking make her feel so…so…angry. She blinked back the tears which had so ridiculously filled her eyes. What on earth was there for her to cry about, or to cause such a huge and painful lump of anguished emotion to lodge so dangerously inside her? She didn't *want* Alex to get in touch with her.

The telephone rang just as she was filling the kettle, making her jump. Her fingers were trembling as she picked up the receiver but the caller was only her mother, ringing to make sure she was all right and to have a newsy chat.

'Ma, has there been anything on the news about a convoy of travellers?' she asked her mother curiously, once she had listened to all her news.

'No. Well, I certainly haven't heard anything, darling,' her mother told her. 'Why, is—?'

'Oh, no reason,' Mollie fibbed. The news blackout, whoever had ordered it, was certainly working.

She was just settling down with a mug of coffee to

read through her mail when she heard the doorbell ring.

It wouldn't be Alex, of course, she reassured herself, but when she opened the door and discovered that it was, instead of feeling the justifiable irritation that she ought to have felt at his dismissal of her message, she could literally feel the giddy, intoxicating mixture of excitement and happiness bubbling up inside her and fizzing dangerously through her veins.

'What are *you* doing here?' she still managed to demand, even though her voice sounded far more huskily soft than sternly disapproving. 'If it's because of the Land Rover, the keys are at the office.'

'I know. I collected them earlier.'

Somehow or other he had managed to step inside the hallway, and to her own chagrin Mollie discovered that she had allowed him to close the door behind himself. Technically, as her landlord, she supposed he did have the right to enter the house without her invitation, and it was probably just because it had been a warm afternoon, and the space in the hall was so limited, that she seemed to be having so much difficulty breathing properly.

'I...I *had* to take it,' she told him defensively as she automatically backed away from him. 'I...I needed...' She swallowed against the emotion which was inexplicably blocking her throat.

'I had to get home...' she told him lamely, unable to bring herself to meet his eyes. 'I had my copy to write,' she added, 'and—'

'I haven't come about the Land Rover,' Alex interrupted her. 'I've brought your car back for you. I had it taken into the garage to have the tyres changed.'

Her *car*... Mollie's eyes widened. What on earth was the matter with her? How could she have forgotten so totally about it? She could feel her face starting to burn with self-conscious colour.

'Er...I...you...didn't need to do that,' she told him defensively. What on earth would he think if he knew that she had virtually forgotten all about her car? That her mind, her thoughts, her feelings had been so totally and inappropriately focused on him and last night virtually all day that she simply hadn't given the car a single thought? 'I...I fully intended to make arrangements to have it picked up myself,' she lied.

'The police have put a cordon round the area, which could have made it difficult for someone to get in to collect it. Since I had to drive out there anyway, it seemed a good idea to get it sorted out whilst I was there.

'Besides,' he added wryly, 'if you'd left it there much longer I have a feeling that there might not have been much of it left to pick up...'

'That's typical,' Mollie exploded, glad to have an excuse to give vent to her dangerously emotional feelings. 'Go ahead, condemn them, brand them all as...as not being capable of having the same standards as people like you... Bob was saying earlier that there's a news blackout on them being here. What are you planning to do? Organise a vigilante band to drive them out and make them leave, using force if necessary? That's—'

'Don't be ridiculous,' Alex interrupted her frostily.

'Why did you go to see them there? Not to make a welcome speech, I'll bet,' Mollie jeered.

'You seem to forget—my stepsister is there, apart

from which it is my land and they're on it. Both the chief inspector and I thought that it might be worthwhile trying to negotiate with them. If they could have been persuaded to leave now, before too much damage is done and local feelings start to run too high, the police were prepared to give them an escort to Little Barlow.'

'Very altruistic,' Mollie sneered, and then challenged him. 'Your altruism wouldn't have anything to do with the fact that they're on your land, and that you know that legally you can't evict them, at least not yet, would it?'

'You may call it altruism,' Alex told her quietly, ignoring her sarcasm. 'I prefer to call it realism. That site simply isn't any place for them to be.

'Apart from the damage which they're inflicting on the land, there's also the fact that they're introducing a large number of small and potentially vulnerable young children into an area which possesses an unfenced and very deep lake—not to mention heaven alone knows how many other hazards. It only needs one of those kids to eat the wrong kind of berry or mushroom. They're not country-born and bred; neither they nor their parents have the first idea...'

He paused and ran his fingers through his hair, a gesture which Mollie was beginning to recognise as an indication that he was finding it hard to control what he was feeling.

'Some of those poor damned kids...' he began, pushing his hand through his hair in fresh agitation. 'Their mothers...' He paused again and shook his head. 'I can't help thinking that them being there is a tragedy just waiting to happen—that lake...'

'Are you trying to suggest that their mothers aren't fit or caring parents?' Mollie demanded. 'Because if so...'

'No, what I'm saying is that having upwards of a couple of hundred people, many of them young children, living rough in an area which includes a very deep stretch of water is not a good option. Some of those girls...' He paused once more. 'They are girls...'

'Carol, Bob's advertising manager, suggested today that one of the reasons they chose to move into the wood might have been because of Sylvie. *She* seemed to think that she might have suggested the place as a potential site as a means of...'

'Punishing me?' he finished for her. 'What are you trying to suggest...? That if a tragedy *did* happen it would be *my* fault for refusing to take out a court order against Sylvie's mother and trying to get Sylvie made my ward of court? Because, believe me, that's what I would have had to do. My stepmother made it more than plain that she would not allow Sylvie to live with me. According to her, she couldn't do so because of what her friends might think. She didn't want them to start thinking that she wasn't a caring enough mother.

'No, there's more to Wayne deciding to pick on the wood as a good place to stay than him simply acceding to one of Sylvie's suggestions. Even though I admit that initially the idea must have been hers. Only someone with the right kind of local knowledge could have known about the wood. But having said that...'

'Some seem to think the townspeople are concerned that he might be planning to hold a rave...'

'Well, it's certainly a possibility—if only so that he can sell some drugs. But I don't think we need to worry too much about that happening. As I said, the police have the whole area cordoned off now, and they're monitoring all the travellers' comings and goings.'

'They can't stop them from leaving the camp,' Mollie pointed out.

'No,' Alex agreed, 'but for their own sakes they'd be wise to keep a low profile. There's a lot of antagonism towards them amongst the townspeople...'

'Which you approve of, no doubt...'

'Which I most certainly do *not* approve of,' Alex countered acerbically. 'Look, I don't know where you've got this idea that I'm some kind of...'

He paused and shook his head whilst Mollie supplied mock-sweetly 'Don't you? I should have thought it was obvious... Unlike you, *I* judge as I find.'

'Do you...?'

The look he gave her felt like an electric shock jolting through her body.

'Last night...'

'I don't want to talk about it.' Mollie fended him off quickly, instinctively turning away from him so that he couldn't see her face or guess from her expression just what she was feeling. Increasingly, the enclosed space of the small hallway was making her aware of him in all sorts of far too intimate ways.

It was impossible to look at him now, fully dressed as he was, without remembering last night, without inwardly aching for the intimacy of his warm bare flesh against hers, for his hands, his mouth on her skin and hers on his. Only this time…

Helplessly she squeezed her hand into a small fist as she fought to suppress the hot acid tears she could feel burning the back of her throat. This time it wasn't just physical intimacy with him that she craved. This time she wanted emotional intimacy as well. This time she wanted the freedom to whisper to him all the sweet, self-betraying words she had forced herself *not* to say last night; this time she wanted to hear him saying them to her, showing her, telling her with something much more vocal than the low, passionate sounds of pleasure he'd made against her skin last night that what they were sharing meant something special to him, that *she* meant something special to him.

As she recognised just where her thoughts were leading her, Mollie bit down hard on her bottom lip.

Behind her, Alex took a deep breath and then another. God, but she knew how to hurt.

Had she *any* idea just how much she was hurting him?

He wasn't the kind of man who went to bed with a woman just for sex, and, anyway, to describe what they had shared last night as just 'sex' was a desecration, a denial of all that he *knew* it had been—for him at least. And for her? That he had aroused her, pleasured her, there was no doubt, but to leave him this morning as she had done, creeping out like a thief whilst he was still asleep, leaving him to wake up, expecting to find her there beside him, and to find instead that all there was was that curt, cold note informing him that what had happened was something that was best forgotten…

Still, maybe she had done him a favour. If he had woken up to find her in his bed this morning he doubted that he would have been able to prevent himself from telling her how he felt, from admitting that, impossible and unrealistic though it might seem, he had virtually fallen in love with her at first sight and that he had certainly loved her at first kiss…first touch…

Obviously, though, she did not share his feelings. Although why on earth he should love her he had no idea. He had never met a more stubborn, wrong-headed woman in all his life, one so wilfully determined to misrepresent and misjudge him. Nor had he ever met a woman who made him feel the way she made him feel, a woman who made him feel that right now the only thing he wanted to do was to reach out and take hold of her…

Had she any idea how the sweet, womanly scent of her in the small enclosed space of the hallway was driving him out of his mind, how every time he looked at her all he could see…think about…was the way she had been last night? He had *never* experienced anything more erotic than the almost shy way she had admitted and revealed her fantasy to him— unless it was the way she had responded when he had wooed and seduced her into playing out that fantasy with him. But, for him, it had been no mere fantasy. He knew that he would never again enter the Queen's room without thinking of her, without longing for her.

This morning the linen sheets had still borne the imprint of her body, had still carried its scent. It was just as well that Jane was away, nursing her father; she would have been bound to wonder what on earth was going on and why on earth he was sleeping in the Queen's room instead of his own bedroom.

This was torture, torment...unbearable, Mollie told herself in silent emotional anguish. This morning, driving away from Alex, she had thought she had escaped in time. Now she knew she had been wrong. Now she knew that last night had had nothing to do with living out some teenage fantasy with a man who, whilst he aroused her to the point of insanity physically, did nothing for her emotionally at all, and instead that it had had *everything* to do with the fact that from the very first time he had touched her Alex had blasted a hole in her emotional defences so large and damaging that the havoc it had caused could never be mended, that the whole structure of her life had been undermined by it. By him. In short that she had fallen desperately and completely in love with him.

A low groan escaped from her tense throat and immediately Alex was at her side, demanding hoarsely, 'What is it? What's wrong?'

His hand was on her wrist so that she had no option but to turn to face him as she denied huskily, 'Nothing...I'm fine... I...what's happened to your face?' she whispered shakily as for the first time she saw the blood-encrusted gash disappearing into his hairline and the swelling surrounding it.

There was another bloodstain on his sleeve, she noticed, her eyes widening as she saw the tear in the fabric of the checked shirt he was wearing.

'It's nothing,' Alex reassured her.

She had gone a peculiar shade of chalk-white, her eyes enormous in her shocked face. She must be one of those people who couldn't endure the sight of blood, he decided as she started to sway slightly.

'It *is* something,' Mollie protested chokily. 'You've been hurt…what happened?'

As she spoke she lifted her free hand to touch his face anxiously.

'I got caught by a sharp stone—one of the kids at the site…' Alex shrugged.

'A stone…you need to get the cut cleaned,' Mollie told him quickly. 'It could be infected. Your tetanus injections…?'

'Are up to date,' Alex reassured her, adding softly, 'But you're right; it does need some attention. Perhaps I could use your bathroom.'

'I'll do it for you,' Mollie insisted as she quickly led the way upstairs. 'There's blood on your shirt-sleeve as well,' she pointed out. 'And a tear.'

'Yes, I know,' Alex agreed.

They were upstairs now, Mollie guiding him into her bedroom and pushing him down onto the bed with maternal sternness as she instructed, 'You just sit there. I'll go and get some cotton wool and antiseptic.'

Alex did as he was told. From where he was sitting on the end of the bed he could see her moving about the small, pretty *en suite* bathroom, her forehead puckered in a frown as she equipped herself with what she needed.

'This will probably hurt,' she warned him as she returned, carrying a small wicker basket filled with balls of pastel-coloured cotton wool and a bottle of liquid antiseptic.

Hurt... Right now nothing could hurt more than the ache he could feel building in his body and his heart, Alex acknowledged as he dutifully turned his head towards her and closed his eyes as she started to cleanse the cut.

It was Mollie who winced as she wiped the dried blood from the cut and exposed the raw edges of flesh surrounding the gash. Fortunately, it didn't look deep, and so far as she could see there was no dirt visible to the naked eye in it. However, just to be on the safe side, she doused it very thoroughly with antiseptic before placing a strip of sticking plaster over it.

'What about your arm?' she asked when she had finished.

'I'm not sure,' Alex fibbed. 'Could you have a look at it for me? I'll take off my shirt...'

'No...' Mollie began, and then stopped, her face flushing. 'Yes, yes, go ahead,' she corrected herself, a little shakily.

Alex frowned as he removed his shirt. That sharp 'No' had possessed a decided edge of fear. Surely to God she wasn't *afraid* of him, dammit? He simply wasn't that kind of man. No woman had ever had any cause to fear him.

Mollie held her breath as Alex dropped his shirt onto the bedroom floor. His body was so...so beautiful, if that adjective could be applied to a man. It...he was certainly beautiful to her. Beautifully male, beautifully sensual and sexy, beautifully *him*. She ached to reach out and touch him, to retrace the exploratory journey she had made across his body last night, to touch him, taste him, to...

'Are you feeling okay?'

Hastily Mollie pulled herself together and reached into the basket for a fresh piece of cotton wool.

The gash on his arm was much longer and deeper than the one on his forehead, and she frowned as she parted the jagged edges of flesh, but to her relief fresh blood welled up from the cut immediately, clean and red and free from any trace of dirt. Even so...

This time Alex did wince as she liberally doused the area with antiseptic.

'It's for your own good,' she scolded him gently.

'Yes, Nurse,' he agreed mock solemnly, his mouth curling into a teasing smile as he asked her, 'Why do I get the impression that you're enjoying this...?'

Mollie couldn't help it. She could feel herself starting to smile back and began to blush slightly.

She *was* enjoying it, it was true, but not for the reason that *he* supposed.

Just being close to him like this, just sharing this emotive, unexpected intimacy with him, was suddenly something so precious that just experiencing it and acknowledging what she was feeling brought a sweetly hot sting of tears to her eyes.

To disguise what she was feeling she bent her head, and then realised just how close her face was to his arm...how close her lips were to his skin.

It was impossible to stop herself from bending her head just that little bit further and brushing the area just above the cut with her lips.

Alex froze, then turned his head to look at her downbent head as he felt the delicate brush of her mouth against his skin in a kiss so fleeting that if he hadn't actually seen her he might almost have felt he had imagined it, created it out of his own longing for her.

'Mollie.'

As she heard the deeply urgent tone of his voice it was Mollie's turn to freeze, agonised embarrassment holding her rigid as she felt Alex's hands grasp hold of her arms.

'I didn't mean...' she began defensively. 'It wasn't...'

'I don't care what it was or what it wasn't,' she heard Alex telling her roughly. 'Right now, all I care about is this...' And then he was cupping her face and drawing her unprotesting body between his legs, and then he proceeded to kiss her with such fierce, hungry passion that for Mollie it was like being submerged by a tidal wave of pleasure of such immense force that she had no option other than to abandon herself to it immediately, surrendering to it and to him.

Beneath the palm she had no memory of ever having placed against his chest, she could feel the fierce, deep thud of his heart. His skin felt warm against hers and the scent of him was all around her, arousing her, bringing back memories of last night.

'Oh, Mollie, Mollie...I want you so much,' she heard him groaning against her mouth in between kisses. 'Feel how much,' he demanded shamelessly as he took her hand and placed it against his body in the intimate gesture of acknowledged lovers.

As her fingers touched him Mollie instinctively started to caress him, her own body responding to his

arousal. It was as though they had been lovers for a
lifetime and not just for one night, the way their bodies recognised and wanted one another so immediately
and so intensely.

Mollie couldn't remember inviting him to undress
her but she realised she certainly must have done so
because whilst her fascinated wanton fingers caressed
his body, and her lips feathered delicately hungry
kisses along his throat, she could hear him telling her
hoarsely, 'Yes, yes, of course I will,' before groaning,
'God, Mollie, I want you so much that I'm all fingers
and thumbs. I feel more like tearing them off you
than...'

Mollie shuddered helplessly as she listened to him.
How did one tell a man that that was exactly what
one wanted him to do? That suddenly all the politely
correct ideas one had believed one held about the way
a man should behave intimately towards a woman,
about being equal partners, about the fact that as a
grown-up adult woman she was perfectly capable of
undressing herself rather than pandering to any ar-
chaic male fantasy that *he* had the right to undress
her, had been completely and totally swamped by a
need so primeval and instinctive that there was nothing she wanted more than to have him assert his mas-
culinity and demand from her total female surrender
to his desire for her? That suddenly it was a wholly
acceptable and necessary facet of her womanhood that
he *should* want and desire her in such an intensely
masculine way?

She could feel one of the buttons of her shirt give
way as Alex struggled with them.

'If you don't stop doing that,' he warned her as her

fingers continued to stroke him intimately, 'I'll never get this damned thing off without ruining it.'

That was the point when she should have removed her hand from his body and her body from his hands, Mollie would acknowledge afterwards, but that was later, this was now, and instead…instead… She felt the tension in his body as she slid down the zip of his jeans and stroked her hand inside them. The jolt of sensation that shocked through her as she touched his naked aroused flesh was pure liquid, hot, hot female pleasure.

Mischievously she gave him a teasing, provocative smile, pouting her lips in pretend innocence as she saw the frustration on his face as he tried to be careful with her recalcitrant buttons.

'Mollie,' he protested, but the scent of him, the feel of him, the need of him had gone to her head like ripely fermented wine.

'You didn't have this problem last night,' she reminded him provocatively. What on earth had got into her? What was she saying…? But it was too late, and Alex's fiercely exultant cry of male pleasure as he ruthlessly grasped the edges of her shirt and pulled them apart to reveal her breasts was echoed in the thrilling charge of sensation that thundered through her body.

But that was nothing compared to what she felt when Alex cupped her breasts in his hands and buried his face against them, licking, nipping, sucking until she was pushing herself eagerly and rhythmically against him openly moaning her need.

Quickly, Alex finished undressing both of them, shuddering in a mixture of pleasure and need he was unable either to control or to conceal from her as she ran her fingertips slowly up and down him. The sight of him fascinated her.

'Mollie,' Alex growled. 'Have you any idea what it does to me when you look at me like that...touch me like that...?'

'I want to look at you,' Mollie told him huskily, half whispering the words, semi-shocked to hear herself uttering them.

'And I want to look at *you*,' Alex warned her, gently reaching out to part her legs, his hand slipping between them as he started to caress her.

Mollie moaned in soft appreciation of what he was doing, but it wasn't enough, she wanted *him*, deep inside her, filling her.

'Alex,' she whispered throatily. 'Please...'

'Please what?' he whispered hoarsely back.

'Please *now*,' Mollie responded, shuddering in pleasure as he moved over her and then oh, so slowly and deliciously into her.

It was even better than she had imagined. *He* was even better than she had imagined or remembered, and she could already feel her body starting to shiver with pre-orgasmic excitement and anticipation as he started to move strongly and deeply within her.

Mollie reached out to hold onto him, wrapping her legs tightly around him as she abandoned herself to the pleasure they were sharing, building with every rhythmic movement of their bodies. Being with him felt so right, so necessary. It was hard to imagine that there had ever been a time when he hadn't been a part of her life.

'Mollie. Mollie.' He cried out her name in the

throes of sensual ecstasy and release. Mollie felt her own body shudder in convulsive pleasure. She could even feel the hot, explosive surge of his climax inside her own body, and as she did so she couldn't help wondering how it would feel to make a baby with him, to create a new life, deliberately and knowingly, to come together like this with the added dimension of knowing that they were sharing not just an intimacy but an act which would tie them together for all time with the uniqueness of the new life they had created.

Emotional tears filled her eyes. Swiftly she closed them, and as he watched her Alex felt his heart grow heavy. *Why* was she so elusive, withdrawing herself from him, rejecting him almost, just when he most wanted to be close to her, just when he ached to tell her how much he loved her? By closing her eyes he felt as though she was deliberately shutting him out, not just out of her sight but out of her life, her heart, her love.

He wasn't a chauvinist; he could fully understand and respect the fact that a modern woman did not necessarily have to love a man in order to enjoy having sex with him. The problem was that he might not be a chauvinist but he *was* old-fashioned enough to know that he could not reciprocate those feelings. He *did* need to feel love for a woman in order to make love with her and to her.

He smiled grimly to himself as he eased his body away from Mollie's. What would she say if she knew what he had been thinking just now as he'd felt his body reaching release within hers? If she knew just how tempted he had been to whisper to her how he'd felt as though he wanted to give her not just the sexual satisfaction he knew she had reached but more…much more…that he wanted to give her his child?

Wasn't it the woman who was supposed to want to secure the man by conceiving his child, not the other way round? He bent his head to kiss her and then looked at her still closed eyes and changed his mind. What was the point? She obviously didn't want him, love him, as he did her.

Behind her closed eyelids, Mollie felt Alex moving away from her. She must not, she *would* not cry… Not now… There would be plenty of time for her tears later, when he had gone.

'Mollie…' Alex tried one last time.

Determinedly she ignored him, keeping her eyes closed as she reached out to pull the duvet around her naked body and bury her head against the pillow.

Sighing, Alex pulled on his clothes. She was making her feelings plain enough; she didn't want him to stay.

Mollie waited until she heard the front door close after him before giving way to her emotions, crying until she felt sick and light-headed with the force of what she was feeling.

She had done the unforgivable. She had fallen in love with a man who did not, and never would, love her back.

CHAPTER SEVEN

'AND there's a meeting been called in the town hall this evening to discuss what's happening. Ah, Mollie, good morning—or should I say good afternoon?'

Mollie winced as she felt the eyes of her colleagues turn in her direction as she opened the main office door. She had been awake all night, finally falling asleep just before dawn with the result that she had overslept badly this morning. Her head ached and she knew that her face looked puffy and her eyes red. It was still unfair, though, of Bob to make out that she was that late. It was, after all, only half past ten, and not lunchtime as he was implying.

She could see his expression changing from one of irritation to one of concern as he looked properly at her for the first time, at her pale face and red-rimmed eyes. His concerned 'Are you all right?' caused her to dig her nails into her palms to stop herself from giving way to fresh tears. Never had she felt so emotionally vulnerable.

'I...I've got a bit of a headache,' she told him, not untruthfully, whilst the more stalwart side of her nature winced at the feebleness of her excuse.

'Mmm... Well, I was just telling the others that a meeting's been called in the town hall this evening to discuss the problems surrounding the arrival of the travellers and what's going to be done about them. I want you to attend.'

'Yes. Of course,' Mollie agreed, and told him, 'I had hoped to go out to the camp today and interview some of the travellers. I thought it might be a good idea to run some human interest stories about individual members of the group.'

'Go for the sympathy vote on their behalf, you mean,' Bob suggested dryly. 'Well, you're welcome to try, although I doubt you'll be able to drum up much sympathy for them amongst our local readership.

'The off-licence was broken into last night and several cars parked in the town square had their tyres slashed and their windscreens smashed, so local opinion is running quite high against the travellers at the moment.'

'I'd still like to do some interviews,' Mollie persisted doggedly.

Bob gave a small shrug.

'Fine, but don't get *too* carried away,' he warned her. 'You can interview them, but I'm not promising to publish what you write.'

'If I didn't give them a chance to put forward their viewpoint, it would be biased reporting on my part,' Mollie told him passionately.

'All reporting is biased one way or another, and you're a naive fool if you believe otherwise,' Bob told her phlegmatically, but Mollie wasn't in any mood to listen.

She wanted...*needed*...to immerse herself in her work, in a just and demanding cause. She *needed* something to stop her thinking about Alex, to stop her longing for him, aching for him, loving him.

She had been such a fool not to guess, not to *know*

that that feeling she had interpreted as antagonism towards him the first time they had met had really been forewarning. And she had been right to be wary of him. What had happened between them had proved that.

Look at the way he had walked away from her last night, so easily and so uncaringly. It was obvious now that he was just amusing himself with her, just—oh, how she hated the word—*using* her for his own sexual gratification. All right, so maybe *she* had been the one to insist that she wanted nothing further to do with him, but surely after last night he must have realised, seen, guessed, *known* how she really felt.

Perhaps he had, and perhaps *that* was why he had left so abruptly, she told herself cynically.

He was, as she had first supposed, Mollie decided bitterly, a dangerously arrogant and far too male person. A man—selfish, thoughtless, *uncaring*. A complete…a complete *beast*, and if she had any sense she ought to be grateful for the fact that she had been given the opportunity to see him as he really was.

A complete beast maybe. But still the man who had touched her heart, her soul, her body, in a way that…

But no, she mustn't give in to the weakness and danger of such thoughts. She had work to do, she reminded herself firmly.

At first, the policeman on duty was a little reluctant to allow her through the cordon surrounding the camp, but then, unexpectedly, his colleague recognised her car and asked her, 'Isn't that the car that Lord St Otel was arranging to have picked up and repaired yesterday?'

'Yes. Yes, it is,' Mollie agreed, low-voiced.

'It's okay,' he told the other policeman. 'The young lady here is a friend of the Earl's. You can let her through.'

'I'm a reporter—' Mollie started to correct him indignantly, but neither of them was really listening to her, their attention on the next car wanting to pass the checkpoint.

Yesterday's sunshine had gone, to be replaced by a fine drizzle of late summer rain. As she approached the camp site Mollie felt her heart sink when she saw the deep furrows of mud-spattered torn grass that marked the verges at the roadside. She parked her car and got out. The scents of damp undergrowth and woodsmoke mingled in the air, along with other odours she felt less inclined to want to analyse.

The travellers had set up a checkpoint of their own, and their initial reaction to Mollie's announcement that she had come to do some interviews with individual members of their group was one of cynical hostility.

'Wayne said to leave the press to him,' one of them reminded the others.

'Perhaps I could speak to Wayne, then,' Mollie suggested.

He shook his head. 'Nope. He's not here. He's got some business...'

'Sylvie, then?' Mollie asked. 'Is she here?'

'Oh, "yah", *she's* here all right,' another of them sneered.

'Perhaps...if you could take me to her?' Mollie asked him. A group of pre-teenage boys were wrestling on the ground several yards away, their noise disturbing a couple of wood pigeons who flew out of a nearby tree.

'I'm gonna shoot them,' Mollie heard one of them announce, and to her shock he picked up a shotgun she hadn't realised lay on the ground beside them and started to point it at the birds, firing it.

To Mollie's relief, when the smoke cleared she realised that he had missed the pigeons. But what was a boy of that age doing with such a potentially dangerous weapon?

'Something bothering you?' one of the men at the gate asked her challengingly, his eyes narrowing as he turned to see where she was looking.

'He…he seems a bit young to be handling a gun,' Mollie responded uneasily, all too aware how counter-productive it would be for her to antagonise them.

'It's a tough life. He's got to learn to defend himself. You never know these days when you might have to…'

Just as she started to turn away, sensing that the men were going to refuse to let her into the encampment, she suddenly heard Sylvie's voice and watched the other girl come into sight, walking down the muddy, litter-strewn track that led into the wood. She was obviously arguing with the man who was with her, from the sound of their raised voices. Whoever it was, it was plain that he was no traveller.

Tall and bare-headed, his rich brown hair curling in the rain, he was older than Sylvie, probably around about thirty, Mollie guessed, and dressed in the countryman's 'uniform' of waxed jacket, moleskin trousers and walking boots. He was also frowning angrily, his mouth compressed in a tight line as he sud-

denly stopped walking and angled his body across
Sylvie's, so that she too had to stand still, reaching
out to take hold of her upper arm.

'Do you have the faintest idea of what you've
done?' he demanded. 'Look—look at this place. It's
ruined, totally destroyed...'

Mollie heard not just anger but frustration in his
voice; it was plain that he felt very, very strongly
about the wood.

Mollie suspected that if he hadn't been looking so
angry he would be a very good looking man.

'That's your fault, not ours,' Sylvie shot back. 'All
you had to do was provide us with other facilities,
and don't say you couldn't have done. You got them
easily enough when Alex had the game fair two years
ago.'

'Yes, and I had to pay a fortune for them. Besides,'
he added pithily, 'if it's proper facilities you want,
what the hell are you doing here? But we all know
the answer to that one, don't we?' he jeered bitterly
at Sylvie, then told her, 'Well, I hope you're pleased
with what you've done, with the destruction you've
caused. What kind of person are you? What kind of
sick, twisted mind do you possess that you'd want to
do something like this—destroy something that's
taken three years of hard work to get off the ground,
never mind the fact—'

'I did *not* do it for that,' Sylvie denied, and Mollie
could see as well as hear the tears she was trying to
hold back.

'Then why the hell *did* you do it?' he demanded,
almost shaking her.

Both of them looked round as a young woman

called out sharply to a small child who was walking dangerously close to the edge of the lake, swinging him up into her arms and soothing the frightened tears he had begun to cry as he'd reacted to the panic in her voice.

'Can't you at least do something to fence off the lake?' Sylvie demanded passionately. 'You can see how dangerous it is for the little ones. If anything happens to one of them...'

'If anything happens to one of them then the *death* will be on *your* conscience—along with the death and destruction of the wood,' Mollie heard him telling her unequivocally.

When she saw Sylvie's shocked white face she sucked in her breath, longing to intervene but sensing that the man was too caught up in the grip of his own powerful emotions to allow her to do so. What he was saying had some point to it, of course, but couldn't he see how much he was hurting Sylvie? Mollie wondered sympathetically.

'That's not fair...it's not true—' Sylvie began to deny frantically, but he wouldn't let her continue, breaking into what she was saying.

'Of course it's bloody well true. You brought them here. They'd never have found this place without *you*. Without *you* they'd **have** gone straight on to Little Barlow and—'

'It was Wayne who wanted to come here,' Sylvie interrupted him tearfully.

'Don't bother lying to me, Sylvie; I know you too well—remember?' he told her harshly, and released her arm, his face still contorted with anger as he

started to stride towards the mud-spattered Land
Rover parked at the side of the road.

Sylvie was standing watching him, her face ashen,
her arms wrapped protectively around her body.

'I hate you, Ran,' she shouted after him. 'I hate
you...'

'Yeah, I know,' he threw back at her over his
shoulder, his expression suddenly changing as a
Jaguar sports car pulled to a stop at the roadside and
an immaculately dressed woman got out, her dark hair
pulled into an elegant chignon, her make-up as perfect
as her designer clothes.

Despite the fact that there was no sunshine she was
wearing wrap-around sunglasses which she removed
as she grimaced in distaste at the mud.

'Ran, darling, Alex said I'd find you here. I'm
afraid I need your help. That wretched pony of
Sarah's has escaped again... Good heavens, is that
Sylvie?' Giving Sylvie an amused and disdainful
look, and totally ignoring everyone else, she placed
her hand possessively on the man's arm.

'Heavens, what an appalling smell!' Mollie heard
her exclaiming as they walked back towards her
parked car. 'How much longer are these dreadful people going to be staying, Ran? They're a positive
health hazard...'

'Who was that?' Mollie asked Sylvie curiously five
minutes later, when the couple had left in their re-
spective vehicles and Sylvie had recognised her and
come over to her.

'Which one? The woman is the ex-wife of an ex-
pop-star-cum-financial entrepreneur. She moved here
a couple of years ago on the hunt for a second hus-

band. I think originally it was Alex she'd got in her sights, but then she saw Ran...'

'Ran?' Mollie pressed.

'Yes. Ranulf Carrington. He's Alex's estate manager and Anna is rich enough not to need to marry a second time for money. She got millions from her ex. God, Ran is such a pig. I hate him,' she told Mollie vehemently, her face flushing. 'And he's wrong. It *wasn't* my idea that we should come here.'

Mollie watched her gravely as the expressions chased one another across her face.

'Admittedly I *was* the one who told Wayne about the wood. Not deliberately. We were just talking about the estate and Alex one day. Originally, when the site was being developed, I got co-opted into helping. We...Ran and a group of us...had to clear away the undergrowth and clean out the lake. It was...' She swallowed and blinked hard before saying huskily, 'It was fun. I thought then that Ran...'

Angrily she gave a small shrug. 'That's all in the past now. Ran...Alex...they're both as bad—neither of them really wanted me around...they both made that more than obvious,' she told Mollie bitterly, before continuing, 'It's all very well for them to criticise Wayne, but they don't know him like I do.

'When I first went up to university he was there, and he was so kind to me, so...so gentlemanly,' she told Mollie earnestly. 'I know he's got a bit of a reputation, and that Alex's got this bee in his bonnet about Wayne and drugs...' She gave a dismissive shrug. 'But they're a part of modern life. Nobody is forced to take them,' she told Mollie defensively.

'They are if they become addicted,' Mollie felt bound to point out.

What was it that Ran and Alex had done or said to make Sylvie say that they hadn't wanted her around? Mollie wondered compassionately, but she didn't feel she could pry into the other girl's past when it so obviously distressed her.

Sylvie flushed as she looked away from her, unable to meet her eyes. 'Wayne says that if people want to take them they're better off buying them from someone like him who only supplies good-quality stuff...'

'And you believe that? You agree with him?' Mollie asked her quietly, sensing that she was not quite so comfortable with her boyfriend's lifestyle as she wanted to seem.

'I... I... We don't totally see eye to eye on the subject,' Sylvie admitted huskily, 'but Wayne... Wayne's been very kind to me. He respects me,' she added, bridling as she saw the look in Mollie's eyes.

'Oh, you can look like that. I know what you're thinking, what everyone's thinking, but it's not like that. Wayne and I are...we're just friends. He understands that I'm not...that I don't... Oh, what does it matter? I don't care what any of you think,' Sylvie told her fiercely before turning to run away.

'Sylvie, don't go,' Mollie pleaded with her as she watched the other girl disappearing between the haphazardly parked lorries and trailers. But it was no use; the other girl plainly wasn't going to listen to her.

A young woman carrying a plastic container of water swore as she walked past Mollie and stubbed her toe on a half-exposed tree root, chivvying the young children with her to 'Hurry, for Gawd's sake'.

Another couple drifted past, quite obviously high on drugs and oblivious to the rain. No point in trying to talk to them, Mollie decided tiredly.

The 'guards' on the entrance to the site had changed, she noticed as she made her way back there through the mud. A young woman was talking to one of them and Mollie recognised her as the girl she had seen in the bread shop in town the previous day.

She gave Mollie a wary smile, explaining to the men who she was.

'A reporter?' one of them repeated. 'How did you get past the police?'

'She only works for the local rag,' the girl informed him laconically. 'And everyone who reads that already knows that we're here.'

'Yeah, another establishment pig,' another of the guards commented truculently, giving Mollie a dirty look.

'I'm a reporter, and what I write is *always* completely unbiased,' Mollie defended herself fiercely, honesty compelling her to add, 'Although, if anything, my sympathies lie more with you than with the authorities. But it wasn't necessarily the politics of the situation I wanted to discuss. What I wanted was to talk to some of you as individuals, find out why you chose this kind of lifestyle—'

'Oh, you're into the human interest side of things. Right,' another of the men interrupted. 'Women's page stuff...social-issue-type articles... I was studying media stuff myself before I recognised that there was no way I was going to get myself a job. I might have made it to university but I soon learned that that wasn't going to be enough. I didn't know the right people; my father didn't have the right connections,' he continued bitterly.

'Quite a lot of us are disaffected ex-university students,' another of the group informed Mollie in a light drawl. 'We're even thinking of forming our own political party,' he added mockingly.

'That's not such a bad idea,' someone else broke in. 'We'd certainly do a better job of running the country.'

Suddenly they were off, passionately involved in what they were telling her. Quickly Mollie started to make notes and to listen.

Not all of their views were sympathetic to one another, she recognised as two of the men became involved in a heated argument, and it quickly became apparent to her that the travellers were made up of several very different groups of people. The common thread holding them together was the fact that they felt disenfranchised from everyday modern life in one way or another—either because they could not find work or because their beliefs meant that they followed a different ethos.

Some of their views Mollie sympathised with, some she could not, and when the subject of drugs was raised she found herself having to bite on her tongue to keep her own thoughts and views to herself. What was becoming plain to her, though, was that in the main the travellers were genuine in their beliefs and their determination to win the right to live their lives as they wished to live them.

'This "I'm the Lord of the Manor" business, and

"I own the land"—that's crap,' one youth told her passionately. 'The land cannot be *owned* by any individual and we intend to show the establishment that when it comes to rights theirs are a load of rubbish. The land belongs to *all* of us.'

She only wished that Alex were here to listen to this, Mollie decided vengefully. It would do him good...cut him down to size...make him see that he was, after all, just another ordinary human being instead of believing that he was something somehow special.

Alex. She could feel her concentration starting to wobble. Instead of listening to what was going on around her she was starting to think about Alex again, to remember...

'Look, Wayne's got his own agenda to follow; you must be able to see that.'

Abruptly Mollie made herself focus on what was being said and the argument that appeared to have broken out between two of the men in front of her.

'Wayne doesn't mean any harm and—'

'He's a pusher,' the first man retorted bluntly. 'And in my book that means he's bad news.'

'You're being too hard on the guy,' another man interrupted. 'So he supplies drugs. Someone's got to do it...'

'Have they?' the first man demanded bitterly.

'My cousin died after taking Ecstasy... His first time...'

'It happens.' The other man shrugged dismissively. 'He was unlucky. His number came up...'

'Anyway, how come Wayne can come and go as

he pleases whilst the rest of us are stuck here?' someone else chimed in.

'He's got in with the cops, that's how,' someone
else replied. 'I saw him talking to one of them last
night.'

'Probably offering to supply them,' someone else
suggested with a grin.

Frowning, Mollie closed her notebook. It *was* odd
that Wayne was obviously able to move around freely,
but she doubted that there was any point in trying to
question him on the subject. She gave a small shiver
which had nothing to do with the damp dripping down
her neck. Despite Sylvie's championing of him, she
didn't like or trust Wayne.

But, she reminded herself stalwartly, he *was* a key
figure within the group, and from what she had heard
possibly its leader. That being the case, it would be
unprofessional of her not to at least try to interview
him.

'When will Wayne be back? Does anyone know?'
she asked determinedly.

One of the men tapped the side of his nose and told
her, 'What Wayne does is his own business and he
don't like anyone else interfering in it, see?'

'I simply wanted to interview him about the
group's decision to stop here instead of travelling on
to Little Barlow,' Mollie returned, standing her
ground, frowning as one of the men at the back of the
group turned and whispered something to one of the
others that she couldn't hear.

'I'll come back later,' she announced firmly. 'Perhaps if one of you would mention to him that I'd like
to talk with him.'

Without giving them any opportunity to refuse, Mollie quickly turned on her heel and walked back through the thick mud towards her car.

Her face prettily contorted with the effort she was putting into creaming the fat and sugar together for the chocolate cake she was baking, Mollie paused to glance at the kitchen clock.

Four p.m. The meeting wasn't due to start until seven, which meant she had three hours yet. Three hours of which she was determined not to spend a single second, not even a single millionth of a second, wasting her time thinking about that lordly arrogant and far too wretchedly male man, the Earl of St Otel!

The Earl of St Otel! For goodness' sake. Just say, for instance, just for the sake of exercising her imagination and for no other reason whatsoever, she assured herself quickly, that she was to take what had happened between them to an implausibly and impossibly good old-fashioned supposedly happy ending... Could she really see herself carrying the appalling weight of the name?

Scarlet-cheeked, Mollie suddenly recognised that she had dribbled it out on the worktop with the flour she was using for baking her cake.

A *chocolate* cake.

Furiously she beat the mixture, and then stopped. Her mother made chocolate cake whenever *she* was upset about anything, for goodness' sake. Mollie had always known, when chocolate cake was served at home, that something had upset her mother and disturbed her normally calm and equally gentle nature.

'But why?' she had once asked her on a home visit

from university, ignoring her mother's rueful look as she'd scooped the gorgeously sticky and rich topping off her slice of cake with her finger. '*You* don't even like chocolate cake.'

'I know. There's just something about making it.'

'Must be something to do with all that beating,' Mollie had suggested teasingly.

'Mmm...maybe,' her mother had replied. 'Your grandmother always used to make it when *she* was upset. But then for her, having gone through a war, chocolate cake was an indulgence and a luxury.'

'Comfort baking,' Mollie had offered knowingly.

'Something like that,' her mother had agreed.

Frowning fiercely, Mollie started to sieve the flour into the mixture. It was a sobering, indeed almost a lowering moment of unwanted self-awareness for her to recognise that she was repeating a family pattern, and yet, at the same time, there was something undeniably comforting in that knowledge, even for someone as independently minded as herself.

Her frown abruptly deepened.

But did that mean that in twenty or so years' time *her* daughter would be standing over a bowl of cake mixture venting her negative emotions?

Her *daughter*. Subtly her expression changed, her face softening, illuminating, her lips parting in a totally womanly knowing smile.

She would look like her father, of course, possess all of his stunning good looks, but in a truly feminine way, and he would adore her and spoil her and then accuse her, Mollie, of being the one who was too indulgent with her. He would teach her how to fish and swim, and turn her into a complete tomboy, and then be devastated, bewildered and totally besotted the day she came downstairs in her first 'grown up' and feminine outfit.

He would hate her boyfriends and turn into an ogre overnight—at least in *her* eyes—and he would be the one who would be fighting not to shed an emotional tear when she eventually came to leave home. She would refuse to use the title, of course, but be secretly proud of the tradition of history she had inherited and...

Angrily Mollie sighed as first one tear and then another fell onto the worktop. Miserably she brushed them away. Why on earth was she crying? Alex wasn't the man for her.

He represented so much that she disliked, despised, but then they did say that the best way to change something was to work on it from within.

According to Bob, Alex was a very forward-thinking and liberal land-owner, and a compassionate and caring human being—a man who had banned hunting over his land and who put the interests and welfare of his tenants very high on his agenda of what was important to him, a man who did not trade on the rank and privilege he had inherited, but who rather used them to benefit others, a man who...

A man who had *no* role to play in *her* life, nor her in his, Mollie reminded herself sharply.

Quickly she started to spoon the mixture out into the ready prepared tin. The purpose of baking this cake was to stop herself from thinking about him, not to encourage her to do so, she told herself severely as she automatically scraped the spoon around the bowl and then started to lift it to her lips.

Licking the raw cake mixture off the spoon after her mother had finished baking had always been one of her favourite childhood treats, but now the rich, sticky mixture cloyed. She had lost her taste for the simple pleasures and treats of childhood, she recognised sadly, and as for fantasising about introducing them to her daughter…Alex's daughter…

The bitter-sweetness of the pain that lanced her heart made her catch her breath in anguish.

What was the point of tormenting herself like this? There was *no* point. None at all.

CHAPTER EIGHT

MOLLIE tensed as her telephone rang, but it wasn't Alex on the other end of the line, she realised as she recognised Bob's voice.

'I'm just ringing to let you know that tonight's meeting has been brought forward by an hour,' he warned her. 'And it looks like half the town's going to be attending. Feelings are running pretty high over the travellers.'

'Thanks for letting me know,' Mollie told him, and assured him, 'I'll make sure I'm there early. That way I might be able to get some off-the-cuff comments from people before and after the meeting.'

'Good idea,' Bob approved.

Good idea it might be, but it meant that she was going to have to leave the kitchen looking dreadfully untidy, Mollie recognised as she removed her cake from the oven. She was not going to have time to clean up after her baking session if she was going to make good her promise to get to the town hall ahead of the meeting starting.

When Mollie reached the town square she discovered that it was busier than she had expected, with a steady stream of people heading purposefully for the town hall. When she stopped and informed them that she was reporting on the meeting for the local paper they proved willing, and in some cases even eager, to express their feelings about the arrival of the travellers in the area.

'They should be moved on,' one young woman told Mollie roundly. 'My kids were part of the school work party that helped replant that wood. My Daisy was heartbroken when she heard at school what had happened. The whole class had been promised that they could visit it next spring, when the primroses are in flower.

'What's the point of us trying to teach them a sense of community and shared responsibility for their environment if outsiders can come along and do something like this?

'I'm sorry,' she apologised to Mollie. 'But we moved into the area to give our kids the benefit of a country upbringing. My husband had to take a much lower paid job so that we could move here, and now this. It's exactly the sort of thing, the sort of *attitude* we're trying to protect them from. When there's a proper site for them at Little Barlow, you just can't help thinking that they've chosen the wood on purpose. That they actually want to destroy it...'

'I'm sure that's not the case,' Mollie protested.

'Isn't it?' the young woman asked her grimly. 'I've heard that it's that little madam, Alex's stepsister, who brought them here. Typical of the kind of thing she'd do. She's a real troublemaker.'

The point of view expressed by the younger woman about the desecration of the woodland was one that Mollie heard repeated over and over again in a variety of forms during the next half an hour as she interviewed people arriving for the meeting.

Some had other views to express, of course—concerns about livestock and crops from the farming community and concerns about the vandalisation of their property from the town's shopkeepers.

Even the publican Mollie interviewed seemed to view the travellers' arrival as a threat rather than a benefit, and that despite the fact he agreed that they had dramatically increased his business.

'But what's the good of that when they're driving away the locals? They won't be staying long, and where will I be once they are gone? Three fights last night we had, and half of them spaced out on God knows what.' He shook his head, walking away from Mollie and into the town hall.

Out of the corner of her eye she saw a familiar Land Rover pull up and her stomach muscles clenched.

Busying herself, so that she wouldn't have to look at him, she deliberately kept her back towards Alex as she determinedly interviewed an elderly woman who patently did not want to be interviewed. She responded truculently to Mollie's questions and then turned away from her to catch Alex by the arm as he started to walk past them.

'What's going to be done about them?' she asked him anxiously. 'My cottage is right at the end of town and I'm living there on my own.'

'Don't worry, Mrs Liversidge,' Mollie heard Alex telling her gently. 'Ran is keeping an eye on that piece of road, although I doubt you'll have any trouble. It's on the opposite side of town from the wood.

'Mollie.' He acknowledged her quietly, indicating that the elderly woman was to precede him into the hall and thus forcing Mollie to stand beside him.

Once the woman had done so, Mollie made to dart forward, anxious to put as much distance between them as she could and even more anxious to ensure that Alex knew that so far as she was concerned what had happened between them was now in the past, that she had no desire whatsoever to have anything more to do with him and that she most certainly had *not* been hanging around outside the hall like some love-struck teenager, just waiting for an opportunity to see him.

Once inside the hall, she fully intended to stay as far away from him as she possibly could, but Alex, it seemed, had other ideas, catching hold of her arm when she would have darted away.

'Let go of me—' she began, but he silenced her.

'I understand that a chair's been reserved for you on the stage,' he told her coolly.

'If you—' she began again, but once more he refused to allow her to finish.

'Bob arranged it. He thought you'd get a much clearer picture of what was going on from the stage rather than from the floor.'

Mollie looked away. Bob was right, of course, but the last thing she felt able to cope with right now was being in any kind of close proximity to Alex. *Any* kind at all.

A little to Mollie's surprise, the meeting opened on time—thanks to Alex, she was forced to acknowledge as she observed the extremely skilled and tactful way he got things started and then proceeded to field everyone's questions. He answered them calmly and concisely, clearly intent on taking as much heat out of the situation as he could, Mollie reluctantly had to concede, and even at one point put forward some arguments on behalf of the travellers, who, not unnaturally, had not chosen to be represented at the meeting.

It was sheer professionalism that made her write down that fact, Mollie acknowledged, gritting her teeth as she recorded his comments.

'Never mind *their* needs, what about ours?' someone shouted angrily from the audience when Alex had finished.

'The town isn't safe any more. And what's being done about it?'

'The police have got the area sealed off,' Alex responded calmly.

'Sealed off, maybe, but that doesn't stop them coming into town to cash their giros and cause trouble. If the police can put roadblocks up to stop them, why can't they move them on? That's what we want to know. It's your land. You could get a group of men together and...'

'Break the law?' Alex intervened dryly.

'*They're* the ones who are breaking the law,' someone else called out from the audience. 'The law should be on our side, not theirs.'

'There are certain legal moves we *can* make,' Alex agreed quietly. 'But they take time. Meanwhile, the police are trying to do everything they can, first of all to stop any more travellers from moving into the area to join them—which is the reason for the roadblocks—and secondly to keep things as quiet and peaceful as possible whilst they *are* here, and it's to this end that I would like to ask for your help.

'I *know* things aren't easy for you, and I *do* understand your fears and concerns and your anger, but hopefully it shouldn't be too long now before we can start to make some progress. The police and the local authority have been busy trying to arrange talks with the leaders of the travellers to see if we can persuade them to move on voluntarily.'

'Why waste time talking to them? All *we* want is to get them shifted…'

As the arguments flew, Mollie wrote busily.

'When exactly are these talks with the travellers going to take place?' someone asked Alex challengingly.

'Hopefully very soon now,' he responded firmly.

It was late when the meeting finally broke up. Mollie had to wait for the hall to start emptying before she could begin to make her own way to one of the exits. Alex, she realised, was deep in discussion with the chief inspector—not that she had expected him to make any move to delay *her*. Why should he? He would want as little to do with her as she did with him.

She wondered what his precious tenants and all his other admirers would think of him if they knew how he had used her. They wouldn't have such a high opinion of him then, would they?

Throughout the meeting he had consistently refused to criticise the travellers, or to give in to people's angry demands to use force and, in some cases, even violence against them, and if she hadn't known better she would very easily have been deceived into being impressed by the way he had behaved. But she did know better. And anyway it was impossible for *any*

man to be as high-minded and nobly motivated as
Alex affected to be, especially someone with his background, his rank and privilege. He was a hypocrite
and she hated him... Hated him...

'Mollie...'

Deeply involved in her own churning emotions and
thoughts, Mollie hadn't realised that Alex had seen
her leaving the hall. He must have cut across the room
from the opposite direction to have caught up with
her so quickly, she acknowledged as she glared angrily at him, glad of the covering darkness outside the
building to conceal her hotly flushed cheeks.

Her heart was thudding as though she had run a
race and where his hand was resting restrainingly on
her arm she could feel his warmth. Helplessly her
body started to react to it—and to him.

'I've just been talking with Jeremy Harrison, the
chief inspector. He tells me that you're planning to
interview Wayne.'

'Yes. As a matter of fact I am,' Mollie confirmed,
gallantly trying to ignore the depressingly sharp plum-
met of her heart when she realised that Alex had *not*
approached her for any personal reason. 'Although
how on earth he knows about that, or why...'

'He knows because it's his business to know,' Alex
told her quietly. 'Mollie, I don't think interviewing
Wayne would be a good idea...'

'*You* don't think?' Mollie exploded. 'So I was
right,' she told him furiously. 'I *knew* that everything
you said back there was simply a front, that really
underneath you feel *exactly* the same resentment and
hostility towards the travellers as everyone else
around here,' she accused him. 'All those things you

said about being tolerant and trying to see their point of view were just so many…just lies—like—'

'They were *not* lies,' Alex interrupted her bitingly, running a hand through his hair in a tell-tale gesture as he added, 'My God, of all the irresponsible, bigoted little…'

'Me…irresponsible and bigoted?' Mollie burst out. 'If you're so altruistic and fair-minded then just *why* are you trying to prevent me from interviewing Wayne and giving him the opportunity to put his side of things in print? You're just like everyone else. You're just trying to protect the status quo…*your* status quo,' she stormed at him.

'You couldn't be more wrong,' Alex told her grimly. 'What or rather who I'm trying to protect is *you*…'

'You trying to protect me? Hah! I don't believe you,' Mollie retorted, eyes flashing storm signals at him. 'If that was the case you wouldn't have—' Just in time she stopped.

'If that was the case I wouldn't have *what*?' Alex demanded, but, thankfully, before he could pursue the subject any further someone came up to him, wanting to talk with him, their presence allowing Mollie to escape whilst his attention was deflected away from her.

Ten minutes later, walking through the balmy night air towards her house, she paused to breathe in the late summer scent of some night-scented stocks in the garden of a pretty half-timbered house. An old lady who lived near her paternal grandmother had grown them and their scent was one she remembered from her childhood.

There had been a very similar elderly woman at the meeting tonight, and she had spoken very evocatively and emotionally of how she had felt on seeing the wood restored to the beauty she had remembered it possessing as a girl.

After reflecting on how sad, how tragic in many ways it was that instead of enhancing the lives of those around it such beauty should have come to be the focus of so much human anger and aggression, Mollie continued on her way.

Oddly, instead of feeling triumphant and vindicated that Alex had revealed himself to her in his true colours through their recent conversation, what she actually felt was a peculiar and distinctly painful sense of loss and sadness.

What was *wrong* with her? Surely she knew better than to have fallen into the trap of actually believing him, of actually beginning to put him on something of a pedestal, of allowing even the tiniest corner of her mind to think and feel that...?

That what? That she had been wrong about him? Impossible—as he himself had just proved.

The house was in darkness as Mollie unlocked the front door. Pausing briefly in the hallway, she snapped on the light.

The door to the kitchen was slightly open, and a draught was coming into the hallway, almost as though she had left a window open. But that was impossible. Surely she had closed them all before she went out?

A little uneasily she walked into the kitchen, and then froze as she crunched over broken glass.

Reaching quickly and unsteadily for the light

switch, she gasped in shock as she saw that someone had broken one of the kitchen windows.

Who? Though she knew on whom local opinion—to a man and a woman—would put the blame. Shakily she picked her way through the broken glass to the window.

'I'm sorry. I didn't mean to make such a mess, but I thought you'd be in... And then when I found you weren't... I'd forgotten about that damn meeting, and I was desperate so...'

As she recognised Sylvie's voice Mollie felt her earlier apprehension flood out of her to be replaced by a righteous and relief-induced surge of shocked anger as she whirled round to face the other girl.

'What on earth...? *Why* on earth—' she began, only to stop when she saw not only the younger girl's tearstained face but, even more disturbing, the huge bruise which was beginning to darken her left eye and cheekbone.

'Don't. Please don't say anything,' Sylvie pleaded tearfully with her. 'I'm sorry. I'm sorry...' she began, only to break down in huge gulping tears as she gave up trying to speak and buried her face in her hands, her whole body shaking with the tears she couldn't control.

'It's all right. It's all right,' Mollie assured her immediately, and for the second time in twenty-four hours assumed the maternal mantle of her own mother, instinctively taking Sylvie in her arms and holding her gently as she tried to comfort her.

'No. It's not all right,' Sylvie wept. 'Nothing's all right. Everything's bloody well awful, and I can't...'

'Look, let's get you upstairs.'

'Mollie, can I stay here? I don't want to go back to the camp. He—' She stopped and bit her lip.

'You mean Wayne?' Mollie guessed protectively.

But Sylvie shook her head.

'No, it's not Wayne,' she told her. 'It's—' She stopped again.

Of course it was Wayne, Mollie decided, and she, silly little fool that she was, was no doubt trying to protect him. But Mollie sensed that now was not the time to take her to task for her foolishness. She thought she had seen a trace of blood on the younger girl's cheekbone, beneath the rapidly purpling bruise, and if that *was* the case it made sense to get her upstairs, where she could wash and cleanse any cut and perhaps find out a little more about just what had happened.

'This is all Alex's fault,' Sylvie sobbed as Mollie led her upstairs.

'Ouch,' she protested a few minutes later as Mollie cleaned her bruised face. 'That hurt.'

'I'm sorry, but the skin is broken and you don't want to get an infection in it,' Mollie chided her severely.

'I didn't mean to break in,' Sylvie told her a little later, when they were sitting at either side of the fire in Mollie's small sitting room. 'I just wanted someone to talk to and I'd heard someone in town mention that this was where you were living. I'd forgotten about that wretched meeting. It was hard enough getting through the police cordon.

'It's all over with me and Wayne,' she told Mollie. 'He's…that's what I wanted to talk about. I thought…I didn't mean to break the window. I just panicked when you weren't here. There wasn't anyone else I could go to.'

She saw the look in Mollie's eyes and told her defensively, 'I know what you're thinking, but I couldn't go to Alex. He wouldn't have understood. He never has. After all, he's the one who... I found out today that it's true about Wayne, that he is involved in supplying drugs—much more so than I had believed. I overheard him telling someone and when I challenged him about it he...'

'He hit you?' Mollie suggested, her own voice tightening with angry distress.

'He was so angry,' Sylvie told her shakily. 'He wanted to know how much I'd overheard...he frightened me... You won't tell Alex, will you?' she begged Mollie. 'Promise me that you won't tell him.'

As she spoke she was looking wildly towards the door, and, fearing that if she didn't give Sylvie the promise she was demanding she would simply take flight and possibly, no doubt disastrously, end up going back to the man who had abused her, Mollie nodded and confirmed, 'I won't tell him.'

'I'm hungry,' Sylvie told her, her mood abruptly changing as she asked Mollie winningly, 'Could I have some of that chocolate cake? It's my favourite.'

There might only be a few years between them but, watching Sylvie devour the chocolate cake a few minutes later, Mollie felt immeasurably older than her, and somehow responsible for her.

'Is it okay if I stay here tonight?' she asked Mollie after she had finished eating. 'That cake was gorgeous. Did you make it?'

'Yes, you can stay, and yes, I made it,' Mollie confirmed.

'Chocolate cake is Alex's favourite too,' Sylvie told her slyly, starting to smile as Mollie's face burned bright pink.

'Your stepbrother's likes and dislikes are really of no interest whatsoever to me,' she told her stiffly.

'Really?' Sylvie asked her *sotto voce*. 'Then how come you've written his name in flour in the kitchen?'

Mollie's face burned an even deeper shade of pink. Why on earth hadn't she cleaned away that betraying doodle before going to the meeting?

'I did it, that's all. It doesn't mean anything,' Mollie defended herself quickly.

'Are you in love with him?' Sylvie asked her perkily.

'No, I'm not,' Mollie denied, but knew that Sylvie guessed she was lying.

'It's heaven being here,' Sylvie told her, wriggling her bare toes in front of the gas fire Mollie had lit to take the late-night chill off the sitting room. 'I'm never, ever going to take running water for granted again. May I borrow your shampoo and wash my hair…?'

Alex had described his stepsister to her as immature, and whilst Mollie could not bring herself to be so critical she couldn't help thinking that Sylvie certainly had a very youthful ability to shrug off problems.

'It's definitely over between me and Wayne now,' Sylvie repeated an hour later, when Mollie's yawns had finally prompted her to acknowledge that it was time for bed. 'Not that it was ever really on between us, if you know what I mean... That is, we were...you know...supposed to be an item, but Wayne never... Not that I'm going to be able to go to my marital bed a virgin, as my dear mother would wish—but it wasn't Wayne who—'

She froze halfway up the stairs, her face paling as they both heard the sound of someone running down the street outside.

'It's Wayne. Don't let him—' she began, her body tensing as she huddled against the wall.

'No, it's not,' Mollie soothed as whoever it was continued to run past the house. 'You're perfectly safe here.'

She only hoped what she had said was true, Mollie reflected half an hour later as she lay awake in her own bed whilst Sylvie slept in the smaller room next door.

From what Sylvie had let slip about Wayne, there was no doubt that she had done the best possible thing in leaving him, but Mollie had a niggling feeling that her own mother, had she been privy to what Sylvie had had to say, would have immediately counselled her to seek her stepbrother's help, protection and advice. But Mollie had given Sylvie her promise not to do any such thing, and besides...besides... She blushed furiously as she remembered the look on Sylvie's face when she had watched Mollie furiously cleaning away that betraying trail of flour.

In the next bedroom Mollie heard Sylvie give a small, whiffling little noise in her sleep. Wearily she closed her eyes. First thing in the morning she would have to find a glazier and get the window repaired, and then she would try to have a serious talk with Sylvie.

Alex, too, was finding it difficult to sleep as he mentally relived the evening's final angry confrontation with Mollie. Of all the impossible, irritating, downright aggravating women, Mollie was...

Groaning, he rolled over and slammed his fist into his pillow. She was the woman he loved, dammit, and if she followed through with this ridiculous and dangerous plan of hers to try to interview Wayne she was going to be putting herself in a potentially very dangerous position indeed.

After the meeting in the town hall, the chief inspector had informed him that the police were now pretty confident of catching Wayne in the trap they had set for him. Their man on the inside, an undercover detective who had infiltrated himself into the travellers' and Wayne's confidence, had managed to get a message to them that Wayne was expecting to meet with his main suppliers who, posing as a foreign TV crew, were going to break the cordon around the camp and bring in an exceptionally large supply of drugs.

It was apparently a plan Wayne had been working on for some time, but the main block to his putting it into action had been his intention to cut out the middle men currently supplying him with drugs and to make a deal direct with the main suppliers, thus potentially making his 'business' even more profitable than it already was.

The problem had been the fact that he wasn't able to take the risk of meeting with the suppliers on any territory currently run by anyone else, which was why Sylvie's throwaway comment that she knew of just the place for the travellers' convoy to stop had caused him such interest.

Due to the potential risk of discovery, the undercover police officer had been unable to warn anyone of what was being planned—the drug-supplying fraternity had a particularly swift and permanent method of dealing with those they considered had double-crossed them—and his only opportunity to make contact had come after the police had surrounded the travellers.

It had been on the strength of the information he supplied to them that the police had decided to allow Wayne to go ahead with his plans, their intention being to catch him in the act of actually taking possession of and paying for the drugs.

'Let's hope it's soon,' Alex had remarked to Jeremy Harrison only the previous day. 'Judging from the mood of the townspeople, I'm afraid if some kind of action isn't taken soon over the travellers there could be a temptation for some of the more hot-headed element amongst them to take matters into their own hands.'

'That's just what we want to avoid at all costs,' the chief inspector had responded grimly, and Alex knew how relieved he had been to be able to inform him earlier this evening that they had received word that the hand-over of the drugs was due to take place the following day.

'We want to keep everyone else out of the area,' the chief inspector had told Alex. 'With something like this there's always a risk of violence, more especially when drugs are concerned. The Drug Squad have had their suspicions about Wayne's activities for a long time, of course, but the difficulty has been pinning anything on him. This time...'

'Mmm...and hopefully once he's out of the way we can set up a meeting with the travellers and see if we can't persuade them to move to Little Barlow.'

'To make the decision to move on themselves before it's made for them,' the chief inspector had offered dryly. 'Well, let's hope they do. The last thing we want is rioting on the town's streets...'

'The last time *that* happened was in 1786, or so the family records show,' Alex had informed him. 'My ancestor at the time complained that the town's gaol wasn't large enough to hold all the miscreants.'

'I know how he felt,' Jeremy Harrison had told him ruefully.

Mollie... Why had she cut herself short earlier without allowing him to find out what she was saying?

Mollie...

Alex gave another groan as he rolled over again.

First thing in the morning he would go down and see her, explain...make her see reason... Make her...

Make her what? Make her love and want him the way he did her? Dream on, he told himself. Some hope...

CHAPTER NINE

HAVING initially overslept, and then had trouble in rousing Sylvie, who had grumbled and protested, pulling the bedclothes up over her head until Mollie had had to resort to fairly shaking her awake, Mollie was not in a very good mood when she heard the sharp rap on the door.

'It's him,' Sylvie told her, dropping the piece of toast she had been buttering and putting down her half-empty coffee cup and staring nervously at the door. 'It's Ran.'

'*Ran?*' Mollie questioned, disbelieving. 'I thought it was Wayne you were afraid of.'

'Yes. Yes, I am,' the other girl agreed. 'But it was Ran... Don't let him know I'm here,' she pleaded with Mollie, getting up and heading for the stairs, freezing in the shadows as they both heard the door-knob rattle.

'Mollie...' an irate male voice called out imperiously.

'It's Alex,' Sylvie breathed. '*He* mustn't know I'm here. Don't let him in...'

Letting Alex in was the last thing she intended to do, Mollie assured Sylvie, and Sylvie escaped upstairs, leaving her to deal with her unwanted visitor and to feel slightly aggrieved that she couldn't take similarly feminine evasive action.

'I was just having my breakfast,' she began coldly as she opened the door.

'Breakfast? At this time?' Alex was frowning as he glanced at his watch. 'It's gone ten...'

'I had a very disturbed night,' Mollie snapped, gasping an indignant protest as Alex took advantage of her ire to step into the hall and march purposefully towards the kitchen.

'*Hey*, you can't go in there,' Mollie told him, darting past him and standing in the half-open doorway, all too conscious of the fact that two people and not one had plainly been having breakfast before his arrival had interrupted them. But her denial and her actions only seemed to increase Alex's determination instead of deterring him.

'Why not?' he demanded, coming so close to her that she could smell the fresh clean scent of soap on his skin.

Shakily she wondered if there was something wrong with her that such a mundane smell could send her positively weak with longing. Her hormones had an awful lot to answer for...an awful lot.

Dizzily she reached out a restraining arm to prevent him from looking into the kitchen and seeing the broken window she had temporarily boarded up with tape and a piece of hardboard. But Alex wasn't looking at the window. Instead he was looking at the table.

Nervously Mollie followed his gaze. Something about the suddenly hard set to his mouth made her heart miss a beat and then start to thud frantically fast.

'You've got someone else with you,' Alex announced flatly, before demanding, 'Who?'

'It's a…a friend,' Mollie fibbed quickly, adding sharply, 'Not that it's any business of yours.'

No business of his. She couldn't have said anything guaranteed to hurt him more, Alex acknowledged. Who was he, this man with whom she had shared her breakfast and perhaps more? And, more importantly, why hadn't she said anything to him about this man…?

As Mollie continued to guard the kitchen door Alex glanced down the hall and towards the stairs.

'No, you're right,' he agreed heavily, looking back at her, his eyes dark and unreadable. 'It *isn't* any of my business.'

He was back out on the street before he realised that he hadn't warned Mollie that the police would not allow her through the cordon to interview Wayne, and that she would be wasting her time in attempting to do so, as well as courting danger. Fortunately the police would no doubt prove far more proficient at deterring her than he had been. But then hadn't warning her about Wayne simply been an excuse, a means of seeing her, of trying to…?

Alex shook his head. The last thing he had been expecting when she had opened the door to him had been the discovery that she wasn't alone, that someone else, another man, was there with her.

Who was he? How deeply involved with him was she? Not *that* deeply, quite obviously, if she could be so warm and passionate in *his* arms. Grimly he swung himself into the Land Rover and started the engine.

'Has he gone?' Sylvie demanded in a whisper as she tiptoed back down the stairs and when Mollie mutely

nodded she asked anxiously, 'You didn't say anything, did you? You didn't tell him I was here?'

'No. I didn't say anything,' Mollie confirmed bitterly.

How dared Alex imply, *assume*, that she had a man
staying here with her? And not just a man, from the
look on his face, but a *lover*. How could he think that
after…when…? Just what kind of woman did he think
she was? she wondered wrathfully. Just because *he*
had no feelings, no emotions, that didn't mean that
she…

Did he really believe that she would have allowed
herself to respond to him the way she had, that she
would have wanted to respond to him the way she
had, if there had been another man in her life? Did
he truly believe that she would have even begun to
give in to the need to express herself to him so intimately—intimately enough to admit to him her secret
teenage fantasy—if there had been another man in her
life with whom she ought more properly to have
shared that confidence? A man who had far more right
to share it with her?

Frowningly she followed Sylvie back into the
kitchen, where the younger girl was hungrily making
herself some fresh toast.

'Mmm…this is good,' she informed Mollie ten
minutes later, licking the last traces of butter off her
fingers. 'You ought to have some.'

'I'm not hungry,' Mollie told her tiredly and truthfully. The mere thought of trying to force anything
down past the painful lump which had knotted in her

throat made her feel actually ill…sick… Sick with the pain of loving Alex.

How could she love him? How could she possibly love someone so patently unworthy of that love?

'You and Alex have had a row, haven't you?' Sylvie guessed. 'He can be horridly stubborn, you know,' she warned Mollie. 'Especially once he gets on that high horse of his. The trouble with Alex is that he's just so damn moralistic that…'

Alex, moralistic? Mollie curled her lip.

'I don't want to talk about it—or him,' she informed Sylvie pointedly, before asking, 'You did say that Wayne was back at the camp, didn't you?'

'Mmm… Why do you ask?' she questioned Mollie warily.

'I need to interview him for this piece I'm doing on the travellers. Without his input the whole article will be unbalanced.'

'You won't tell him that I'm here, though, will you?' Sylvie begged her.

Did she really need to ask? Mollie wondered as her glance was immediately drawn to the girl's bruised face.

'I won't say a word about you or your whereabouts,' she promised.

'He probably won't talk to you anyway,' Sylvie informed her. 'He's trying to set up some kind of meeting with a TV crew.'

A TV crew! Mollie frowned.

'I doubt he'll be able to do that. The police have imposed a news blackout on the situation,' she reminded her.

Sylvie gave a small shrug. 'I'm only telling you

what I heard Wayne saying. He was talking about it to someone on his mobile, just after I heard him telephoning someone else to tell them that he was expecting a big new shipment of drugs.'

'You *must* have had some inkling that he was involved with them,' Mollie told her quietly when she saw her face.

'I knew that he supplied them, yes,' Sylvie agreed. 'But I didn't realise…well, I thought it was just…he was just… I didn't realise he was involved with them in such a big way,' she finished lamely. 'When I first met him at university, it was the done thing to take the odd E; a lot of students did it.'

'You must have realised the risk you were taking,' Mollie told her severely.

'I didn't really think about it,' Sylvie admitted, a little shamefaced. 'It just felt so good to be on my own and independent after living with Ma.' She pulled a face. 'She was just so…so smothering, if you know what I mean. I just wanted to enjoy everything…to live instead of just existing.'

She really was very, very young, and in some ways still very naive, Mollie decided compassionately as she watched her.

'I've got to go out soon,' she told her. 'Hopefully the glazier will be round at lunchtime to repair the window. I'm not sure when I'll be back.'

'I'm not going anywhere,' Sylvie replied, adding with pathos, 'I don't have anywhere to go.'

Firmly Mollie resisted pointing out that, on the contrary, she had a stepbrother, a mother and, no doubt, university accommodation to return to if she so desired.

*   *   *

Mollie frowned as she looked in her driving mirror. She had seen the four-wheel drive off-roader coming up very fast behind her several minutes ago and had immediately slowed down in order to let it get past. Only, unfortunately, the road was too narrow, running between high hedges, and now the driver was flashing his lights and sounding his horn.

In her mirror Mollie could see his face, and that of his companion. Two men, both grim-faced, both wearing aggressively male wraparound tinted sunglasses.

Mollie's hands tensed on her steering wheel. She could practically feel their hostility and impatience. Who were they? Although the four-wheel drive was liberally covered in dust, its number-plate practically obscured, it looked far too expensive to belong to any of the travellers. A top-of-the-range model, Mollie suspected, and fitted with heavy-duty bull-bars.

She gave a small nervous shudder as she imagined how it would feel to have a vehicle like that rammed into the rear of her own much more fragile and vulnerable car, but before she could let her imagination get the better of her she saw that up ahead of her the road was beginning to widen out.

Expelling her breath in relief, she started to pull over to the side of the road just as far as she could, and then cursed under her breath in dismay as she fully negotiated the bend and saw the wider stretch of road ahead of her was blocked by a car parked on the opposite side.

Instinctively she slowed down, glad that she had done so when a man unexpectedly emerged from behind the car, walking out into the road to flag her down.

The police roadblock. Of course, she had momentarily forgotten about that!

A quick glance in her rear-view mirror showed her that the vehicle behind her was also slowing down. Well, at least once they were through the roadblock she could let him set off first and get past her.

When Alex got back to the house, Ran was there waiting for him.

'I don't suppose you've seen or heard anything from Sylvie, have you?' Ran asked him as he followed him towards the estate office.

'No, I haven't,' Alex confirmed, stopping to turn and look at him. 'Why?'

'We had a bit of a confrontation yesterday and it looks like she's left the camp. No one seems to know where she's gone, or if they do they aren't saying— least of all that creep Wayne, who you might have thought would show at least some concern for her! Does she have the *least* idea what she's doing, the little idiot?' Ran fumed as Alex turned, continuing to walk towards the estate office, and he fell into step beside him. 'She ought to be at university finishing her degree, not...'

He paused and shook his head. 'I went back to the camp this morning to see if I could find out anything but there's still no sign of her, and nor is there any sign of Wayne either. Apparently he's gone off somewhere on business. It beats me how he manages to get through the police cordon so easily. *I* had the devil of a job persuading them to let me through.'

'Wayne isn't there, you say?' Alex questioned him sharply.

If Mollie had her lover staying with her then surely the last thing she was likely to do was leave him and go out to the camp to try to interview Wayne, and even if she did…what business was it of his? She was an adult and, as she had intimated to him on more than one occasion, fully capable of running her own life and making her own decisions.

'There's something I've got to do,' he informed Ran curtly, doing an abrupt about-face and heading back to his Land Rover.

'I thought you wanted to discuss next year's woodland conservation plan and the renovations for the Littlemarsh cottages,' Ran protested.

'Tomorrow,' Alex told him, leaving Ran to frown after him as he vaulted easily into the seat of the Land Rover and drove quickly away.

It wasn't like Alex to change his plans, nor to disrupt arrangements.

Sylvie was in the middle of doing the washing-up when Alex arrived at the back door. Since he had already seen her through the window there was no point in denying him access so she made an insouciant attempt at sang-froid as she opened the door to him and let him in.

'Sylvie. What the hell are *you* doing here—and where's Mollie?' Alex demanded, patently unimpressed.

'I didn't have anywhere else to go nor anyone else to go to,' Sylvie informed him, instantly on the defensive. 'I couldn't come to you, not after the last time when you betrayed me and sent me back to my mother...'

'What? That was different. You were still at school then, a child, and I would have been behaving totally irresponsibly if I'd allowed you to stay—never mind the fact that your mother would have no doubt immediately had me hauled before the courts on a charge of child-snatching.'

'I was seventeen.'

'Sixteen...just...' Alex corrected her before repeating, 'Where's Mollie?'

'She had to go out. Look, why don't you sit down and have a piece of chocolate cake?' she invited him, waving the plate tantalisingly under his nose. 'Mollie made it yesterday. I had some last night.'

'Last night? *You* were here last night?' Alex demanded sharply.

Sylvie pulled a face.

'What is this? The Inquisition? Yes, I was here last night. I made Mollie promise not to tell you or Ran, though...I knew what you'd be like.' She gave him a dark glower. '*And* I was right. I suppose now you're going to start lecturing me about how you were right all along and how Wayne...'

'Alex?' she protested when she realised that he simply wasn't listening to her.

'*You* were here last night. It was *you*...' she heard him saying almost under his breath, before absently biting into the piece of cake she had cut and thrust under his nose. One thing she *had* learned from her mother was that the best way to soothe a bad-tempered man was to feed him something he liked...

'You and I need to have a talk—a serious talk,'

Alex warned her. 'But right now... Did Mollie say where she was going?'

'She mentioned something about wanting to talk to Wayne,' Sylvie informed him, wrinkling her nose as she cut a second slice of the cake and nibbled on it herself. 'Mmm... This icing's yummy. Would you like some more?'

Alex shook his head.

'When did she leave?'

'Not long after you were here before,' she informed him, adding with deliberate emphasis, 'She loves you, you know, Alex.'

She saw him stiffen and then glance away from her, as though he didn't want her to see his expression.

She might be young and immature, as everyone kept on telling her, but she wasn't *that* stupid. It was perfectly obvious how Alex felt about Mollie, how they felt about one another.

'Did *she* tell you that?' he asked her curtly.

Sylvie shook her head, her smile widening as she told him, 'But she did write your name in flour when she was baking.'

'She did what?' Alex was quite plainly nonplussed.

'She wrote your name with hers in flour when she was baking—"the Earl and Countess of St Otel", which means she was thinking about you, which means... Oh, never mind, you're a man; you just wouldn't understand,' she told him with a superior feminine smile. 'Just take it from me, Alex, she loves you.

'Have you seen Ran this morning?' she asked him, changing the subject.

'Yes, and he's none too pleased with you,' Alex

warned her. 'He said something about the two of you having a confrontation at the camp.'

Now it was Sylvie's turn to do the looking away as she played with the piece of cake on her plate and asked him, 'Alex, would you help me to change universities? I'm not really sure the course I'm on is the right one for me and…well, I'd like to be somewhere that isn't quite so close… Somewhere…'

'Where your mother can't insist on you going home every weekend?' Alex supplied for her. 'Well, if you're serious about returning to your studies and *sticking* to them, I'll certainly support you in that decision.'

'And talk to Ma?'

'And talk to your mother,' Alex agreed. 'But it's something we'll have to discuss later, Sylvie. What time did you say Mollie left?' he repeated anxiously.

The policeman manning the roadblock couldn't tell Alex anything. He had only just come on duty, he informed him, nor would he allow Alex to go through to drive onto the camp.

'I'm sorry,' he told Alex firmly. 'But those are my orders. *No one* is to be allowed through.'

Nodding, Alex reached for his mobile. He would have to speak direct to the chief inspector and get his permission for the policeman to let him through. He glanced anxiously at his watch. It was over two hours now since he had last seen Mollie.

The full significance of the fact that neither the car nor the man approaching her was displaying any kind of police insignia was lost on Mollie until she was out of the car and standing in the middle of the road, recognising from the expression on the face of the man now standing opposite her that her presence was far from welcome.

'Who the hell are you?' he began as she heard the four-wheel drive's doors opening and the two men getting out.

A panicky nervous feeling invaded her stomach and she had to stifle a craven desire to bolt back to the security of her car. She felt trapped, caught between two equally potentially unfriendly forces, and then her heart sank even further as the passenger door of the parked car opened and Wayne got out.

Determinedly Mollie fought down her growing sense of apprehension that something somehow was not quite right and that she herself was in danger, by calling out, 'Wayne...I was hoping to see you. I wanted to interview you about the travellers...'

'The travellers!'

A nasty little smile curled Wayne's lips as he turned to make some comment that she couldn't quite catch to the man standing watching her—standing, she now noticed, between her and the safety of her car.

'What's going on, Wayne? We don't do business with women. You know that...'

Mollie whirled round. The two men from the four-wheel drive were standing only feet away from her. Claustrophobically, Mollie felt hemmed in. Trapped. Surrounded on all sides by the four men. A small shudder of fear which she fought to conceal ran down her spine.

'She's not a woman,' Wayne responded mockingly. 'She's a reporter...'

'She's a *what*...?'

Now the second of the two men from the four-wheel drive was speaking, his voice harsher, sharper than that of his companion, and although he hadn't been the one doing the driving Mollie knew instinctively that of the four men present *he* was the one who held the real power. It was obvious from what she could hear in his voice what he felt—not just about her sex, or even her presence, but about her professional status.

'Look, man, it's okay,' she heard Wayne telling him, patently enjoying the sense of one-upmanship it gave him to be able to offer such reassurance. 'I *know* her. She won't cause us any trouble, will you, now, Mollie, babe?' he asked her, coming over to her side and slipping his arm around her, hugging her.

Mollie froze, unable to stop her body from betraying her loathing even though she was aware that behind his mirror-lensed sunglasses the passenger from the four-wheel drive was observing her with deadly intentness.

Suddenly he jerked his head in the direction of his companion, the driver of the vehicle.

'Get rid of her,' he told him unemotionally before turning to Wayne and demanding, 'The money?'

'Leave her to me. I'll do it,' Wayne's companion intervened, adding before anyone else could speak, 'I know the area. It will be easier for me.'

'He's right,' Wayne told the others carelessly. 'He's been dodging the police cordons ever since they put them in place.'

The other man paused and then frowned before nodding and telling Wayne irritably, 'Come on, we've wasted enough time. Let's get down to business.'

'Come on, you.'

Mollie tensed as she felt her arm being taken in an uncomfortably firm hold by Wayne's companion and he proceeded to march her across the road.

'I'll leave the car,' he told Wayne. 'The keys are in it...'

'Yeah, meet you back at the camp...alone,' Wayne agreed, giving Mollie a nasty leer before turning his back on her.

'What...what are you going to do? Where are you taking me?' Mollie demanded nervously as her captor bundled her off the road and across some rough ground.

'This way,' he told her, without answering her question, indicating that he wanted her to push her way through a hedge and into the field beyond it.

On the horizon she could see the trees that marked the beginning of the wood. Her heart started to thump frantically.

'*Not* that way,' a soft, menacing voice commanded in her ear when she started to turn towards it.

Not the wood. Then...

'Here,' he informed her, indicating a small steep track that ran across some rough hilly ground. 'But watch your step; the ground's treacherous around here. In fact it's downright dangerous,' he added tauntingly, 'and if you aren't careful you might have a nasty accident, and we wouldn't want *that*, would we?'

They had gone about a hundred yards when Mollie

heard the sound of a helicopter approaching overhead. Instinctively she stopped walking and looked up. At her side she heard her captor curse under his breath and then instruct Mollie tersely, 'Move it...fast...' He turned his head and looked back at where the two cars and their occupants were still clearly visible.

What was it? Why did he want her to hurry?

The helicopter was closer now and had started to circle overhead, coming much closer to the ground. Mollie's heart lifted and started to thud dizzily in relief as she recognised the police insignia on it and then heard someone inside it announce, 'This is the police. Stop where you are...'

Once again, her captor cursed.

'Down. Get down,' he commanded Mollie, and then, 'Run... Move...'

Mollie froze. She had no intention of moving, or doing anything. Not now. Not when rescue was so close at hand.

Appealingly she looked towards the circling helicopter. From the road she could hear Wayne screaming, 'It's a trap...get the cars...' And then, to her shock, one of the men—the one who had been driving the four-wheel drive—produced a gun and proceeded to fire at the helicopter.

'You can't escape. The road's blocked. Give yourselves up...'

'Mollie...run. Fast...'

Mollie gritted her teeth. No way was she going *anywhere* with anyone, not whilst that helicopter was there, promising her the chance of rescue.

She could hear bullets whining through the air and

then she realised to her horror that they were being fired at them…at *her*…

'Down, down…' the curt male voice behind her urged, a forceful hand implementing the command and pushing her down almost flat onto the muddy ground. 'Keep still. Now…crawl…quickly… No, don't lift your head…keep down…'

It was easier to obey him than to fight him even though every small inching movement she made forward was, Mollie knew, taking her further and further away from the rescue promised by the police helicopter. She badly wanted to cry but she didn't dare even do that.

She heard a vehicle coming towards them. Instinctively she tensed and looked round. The four-wheel drive was heading towards them over the rough ground. Above them she saw the helicopter swing round and a man appeared at the open door holding a gun—a police marksman, she recognised with a sharp thrill of fear as she also recognised that the four-wheel drive was heading for them.

'Down. Keep your head down,' she heard her tormentor demanding. They had been crawling uphill, and now, to Mollie's shock, she felt him suddenly give her a sharp push that sent her rolling helplessly down an unexpectedly steep embankment. His final warning words to her were, 'Don't lift your head. Keep it down…down…'

Above her she could hear the loud, ricocheting whine of gunfire; sharp stones and sticks lacerated her arms and twigs tangled in her hair as she bounced helplessly down the slope before finally coming to rest, bruised and out of breath, in a narrow gulley.

Nervously she lifted her head, and then wished she hadn't. Her captor had obviously followed her down the slope. She could see a cut on his cheekbone oozing blood as, virtually ignoring her, he knelt down beside her, expertly assembling what she realised, to her horror, was a fearsome-looking gun.

'Keep down,' he told her threateningly as he saw her move her head. A small shower of stones and debris rattled down the slope, disturbed by the wheels of the four-wheel drive as it skidded into a turn, its driver trying to outmanoeuvre the following helicopter.

She was *never* going to escape, Mollie acknowledged as weak tears of fear filmed her eyes. The man, her captor, couldn't *possibly* allow her to live. Not now that she had seen him assembling that gun with her own eyes, not knowing what she now knew... Oh, Alex...Alex.

The four-wheel drive had disappeared, along with the police helicopter; the air around them was silent apart from the liquid note of birdsong. The man had put down his gun. Mollie looked at it.

The man looked at Mollie. 'We should be safe now,' he told her evenly. 'But just to be on the safe side I think we'd better lie low a little bit longer. Just in case...'

'We should be *safe*...?' Mollie opened her mouth and then closed it again. To her shame her eyes had filled with tears she couldn't hold back.

As the man put down his gun and came over to her, he told her brusquely, 'It's okay, you go ahead,' and then continued, 'I'm Miles Andrews, by the way. Drug Squad.'

Mollie stared at him, tried to stand up and promptly fainted.

'She's okay, but she's still in shock.'

'I'm not surprised...'

Dizzily Mollie tried to pinpoint why the voice, although familiar, should have such an unfamiliar note of light-heartedness and warmth about it. But, although she managed to open her eyes, the moment she did so everything swam so alarmingly around her that she had to close them again.

'Alex.'

Mollie was unaware of whispering his name as she battled with the icy-cold depths of shock which had caused her to collapse. But other ears had heard it and registered its significance.

'She's asking for the Earl,' the paramedic who had arrived with the police helicopter told the inspector in charge of the operation—unnecessarily.

'Yes, I heard,' he confirmed. 'And *he's* been asking for her,' he added, breaking off his conversation with the undercover detective who had been posing as Wayne's right-hand man and who had cool-headedly managed to extract Mollie from her potential danger as well as preserving his own anonymity.

'He's been causing a real fuss at Headquarters since he found out that she'd been caught up in all of this. Demanded to know why the hell she hadn't been stopped at the roadblock.'

'What did you tell him?' Miles Andrews asked him.

Now that the immediate danger was over he felt rather more kindly disposed towards Mollie than he had done when she had thrown all their careful plans into potential disarray by arriving at the meet seconds ahead of the men from whom Wayne had arranged to buy a large consignment of drugs.

'I explained that she was too close to the supplier—that we couldn't have stopped her without alerting the supplier to what was going on and that we'd invested too much in this set-up to risk it going belly-up on us and Wayne getting clean away.'

'Look, if she's not hurt, the best thing we can do is to let him know she's here and release her into his care. He was practically threatening to hire and fly his own 'copter to get to her if necessary when he left, and the chief inspector had to threaten to have him physically restrained and locked in the cells.'

Mollie was vaguely aware of the conversation going on around her, and then of being gently lifted onto a stretcher and carefully placed into the back of a vehicle, but it *was* only vague awareness. She felt too dizzy, too shaky, too involved in coping with the constant shivering that convulsed her and the unpleasant icy coldness that seemed to have invaded her body to summon the strength to really concentrate on anything else.

As the inspector watched the ambulance doors close behind Mollie, he turned to Miles Andrews and told him forthrightly, 'The pair of you were damn lucky... Damn lucky!'

'Tell me about it,' the other man invited ruefully. 'Pity about Alex Villiers, though...'

'Oh, the chief inspector managed to calm him down...'

'That wasn't what I meant,' Miles Andrews corrected him with a wry smile, nodding in the direction of the departing paramedic vehicle. 'She's *my* kind of woman—*all* woman...' he added wistfully.

'We've got Wayne Ferris in custody—be satisfied with that,' the inspector advised him dryly.

CHAPTER TEN

IN HER sleep Mollie whimpered and then trembled, reaching out to drag the bedcovers even closer to her chilled body. In her dreams she was reliving those terrifying moments earlier in the day when she had been in mortal fear of losing her life.

'Alex...' As she whispered his name in her sleep, caught up in the horror of reliving her trauma, her voice held all the remembered pain of knowing she might never see him again, of knowing that no matter how much she cried out for him he could not be there to hold her. But suddenly, inexplicably, her dream changed and he *was* there, holding her, comforting her, telling her that everything was all right and that she was safe.

'Oh, Alex, you're here,' she murmured blissfully, snuggling deeper into the warm protection of his arms, nuzzling the warm flesh of his throat with her lips and then nuzzling it again as she tasted the gorgeous, sensual, ardour-arousing man taste of him.

'Oh, Alex...' she repeated drowsily, cuddling even closer as she whispered in her dream, 'I'm so glad you're here. Hold me close.'

She gave a small, delicious wriggle of pleasure as in her dream Alex complied, tightening his hold on her body and drawing her even closer to his own— so close, in fact, that she could feel the hot satin stroke of his bare skin against hers.

171

A fierce tremor of responsive pleasure shot through her body. Unhindered by the fetters of convention and conscious awareness, she pressed herself as close to him as she could, reaching out to wrap her arms around him and then to stroke explorative and eager fingertips down his back to his waist, and then lower. She could feel his muscles tensing and hear the sharply altered rhythm of his breathing.

'Mollie,' she heard him breathe warningly, but the warning she could hear in his voice was as nothing compared to the sharp command she had heard earlier in her captor's; instead it was honey, liquid with longing, an appeal rather than a command, and just to hear that low, urgent note of need in his voice filled her with a dizzying sense of female power.

'What?' she asked him teasingly, deliberately trailing pretend-absent-minded little kisses all along his collarbone and feeling the flesh rise in small goosebumps where she touched it, his whole body shuddering against hers as he failed to control his response to her.

'Mollie...' He was groaning, now tensing his body against what she was doing to him. But it was too late for him to put up that kind of defence against her, and besides, the hands he could have used to move her away from him if he had really wanted to were moving urgently against her body—stroking down over *her* back and over the pert mound of *her* buttocks before sweeping up over her again and coming to rest against her breasts, gently cupping and shaping them.

She discovered his doing so made her tremble and shiver in sensual pleasure, just as uncontrollably as he was doing himself, as she kissed her way up his throat, making soft little crooning noises of pleasure to him as she did so.

'Mollie…'

He was *still* protesting? But not in the least bit convincingly, Mollie noted sternly as his thumbs rubbed provocatively and successfully against her nipples, causing them not just to harden and to peak but to ache wantonly with the need for him to continue his caresses.

Well, *she* knew how to put an end to that husky, hoarse male litany to be released from the captivity of his growing, increasingly urgent need of her, and without compunction or a second thought she did so, lifting her hands to hold his head firmly against the pillow as she feathered an admonishing kiss against his parted lips before demanding sternly, 'Mollie what?'

'Mollie *this*,' came back the unexpectedly prompt response and then, disconcertingly, she was on *her* back and *her* head was the one being gently clamped to the pillow by Alex's hands, whilst he subjected her mouth to a far more dangerously seductive brand of kissing than she had given him. A *far* more dangerous brand, Mollie acknowledged giddily as she felt his teeth tug on her bottom lip and his tongue slip inside her mouth, caressing every centimetre of sensitively aroused flesh and making her tremble with frantic longing for him to repeat that slow, powerful male thrust of his tongue with her mouth, with his body…with her body and…

Quickly Mollie opened her eyes. *This* was no *dream*. 'Alex,' she whispered in shocked wakefulness.

Immediately he released her, but he didn't move

his body away from hers, she noticed and even more tellingly she didn't try to move *hers* away from him.

She was, she recognised, lying in the Queen's bed at Otel Place. The low embers of a fire glowed warmly in the hearth and through the open window she could see the yellow gleam of the full moon. As she looked uncertainly round, from Alex's face to her surroundings and then back again, the full events of the day came flooding back over her. Her whole body started to shake with remembered terror.

'Shh, it's all right,' she heard Alex telling her gently as he drew her back into his arms, rocking her tenderly as though she were still a child whilst he soothed and comforted her.

'I thought I was going to die,' Mollie confessed shakily to him. 'I thought the man who took me off was going to kill me. Wayne said...'

'He was a policeman working undercover; he would *never* have hurt you,' Alex comforted her.

'I know...he told me,' she agreed. 'I was so afraid...'

'With good reason,' Alex told her sombrely, and as she heard the emotion in his voice Mollie pulled slightly away from his constraining arms to look up into his face.

'If it had been left to Wayne or the other two...' He paused and shook his head before continuing gruffly, 'When I *think* what might have happened to you. I'll never stop blaming myself—'

'Blaming yourself?' Mollie interrupted him. '*You* weren't to blame. I...'

'Yes, I was... I should have stopped you from going out to the camp. I fully intended to, but...but things got out of hand and I was so eaten up with jealousy because I thought you'd spent the night with another man that I… Oh, God, Mollie, if anything *had* happened to you…' He groaned, his hands trembling against her face, betraying the depth of his emotion.

'I thought you were just…just using me, that…'

'*Using* you…?'

Mollie bit her lip as she heard the stunned shock in his voice.

'Well, it seemed to fit in with everything I—' Mollie began defensively, and then stopped.

'With everything you what?' Alex asked her quietly.

'It seemed to fit the…well, you know what I mean. There's your title, and the fact that you and I come from such different backgrounds. You're titled, privileged, wealthy…'

'I'm *titled*,' Alex agreed, 'and, yes, privileged, but privilege carries its own responsibilities and duties. It can be abused, yes, I can't deny that, but *not* by me, Mollie.'

'I know, I know… I knew that all the time really, but I was afraid. You weren't…I wasn't ready to fall in love, Alex,' she told him defensively. 'Not with *anyone* but most especially not with someone like you.'

'So you defended yourself against doing so by casting me in the role of the villain…the archetypical wicked squire. Is that it?' he asked her wryly.

Mollie hung her head.

'I had to. You seemed too…too good to be true, and I was afraid,' Mollie admitted openly.

'Afraid of what?' Alex asked her gently.

'Afraid of loving you,' Mollie told him. 'I had it all planned—the career I was going to have, the places I was going to go to, the front-page headlines I was going to write...'

'And loving me means that you can't do any of those things?' Alex questioned.

'Loving you means wanting to be *with* you, wanting to stay with you, wanting to have your children and wanting to be with them, to stay with them,' Mollie said softly.

How and why she had come to be here in bed with Alex, what the future held, what the past held, were suddenly unimportant issues as she looked into his eyes and read the message there.

'I thought it was just a dream, being here with you,' she told him unsteadily. 'But it isn't and I'm glad, because dreams are no substitute for reality...'

'No,' Alex agreed soberly as he bent his head towards hers. 'They aren't.'

'Have you any idea how much I love you?' he whispered.

'Some,' Mollie admitted, stroking her fingertips lovingly against his jaw.

'No, not merely *some*,' Alex corrected her sternly, before catching hold of her hand and pressing his mouth hard against its palm, making her whole body quiver with delight—a delight which was heightened almost to the point of a delicious form of subtle torture as he slowly began to suck on her fingers.

'Not merely *some*,' he repeated sternly when he had finally released them. 'I love you completely, utterly, totally—through this life and beyond it,' he informed her rawly. 'I love you more, much, much more than any amount of rank, privilege or wealth, Mollie. So much so that... It *is* possible for a peer to renounce his or her title,' he told her, completely serious.

Mollie caught her breath, guessing what he was leading up to.

'You would do *that* for me?' she asked him breathlessly, her eyes widening.

'I would do that for *us*,' Alex corrected her softly.

Mollie stared up at him. The thought that he was willing to renounce not just his inheritance, nor even his right to the title he had inherited, but so many generations of formality, history and privilege out of love for her, quite simply took her breath away.

Took her breath away and left her feeling awed and humbled, Mollie acknowledged, and if Alex was prepared to make such a sacrifice for her, out of love for her...

'But what about this house, the estate—everything?' she asked him uncertainly.

'I have a cousin—a second cousin to be precise,' he told her. 'He's older than me, and unmarried, but as the next in line everything would automatically pass directly to him.'

'What—what does he do? Where is he now?' Mollie asked him huskily, moistening her lips as she looked around the room.

A queen had slept here, one of the most famous and, by repute, one of the strongest woman rulers the Western world had ever known. Rather than share her inheritance, her power with anyone else, she had renounced her right to marry, to produce children of her own. She had placed duty above love. Mollie tried to imagine how it must have felt to be such a woman.

How lonely this bed must have felt as she lay alone in it without love.

'He's a historian,' Alex told her, adding ruefully, 'And for the last couple of years he's been urging me to marry and produce a family.'

'If he's elderly then he won't be able to run the estates, to care for people's welfare the way you've done, will he?' Mollie questioned him worriedly.

'He can employ people to do that for him,' Alex told her quietly.

'Maybe, but they won't—' Mollie stopped and bit her lip. They wouldn't necessarily be motivated by Alex's sense of duty and responsibility; that was what she had wanted to say. To them it would simply be a job, whereas to Alex it was a vocation, a sacred trust almost. She remembered the look she had seen in people's eyes when they'd talked about Alex, the faith and trust in him that she had sensed.

'I can't ask you to do that,' she told him huskily.

'You *haven't* asked me,' Alex corrected her. 'It's my decision. Love is a two-way thing, Mollie.'

'No, it wouldn't be right,' Mollie said, shaking her head, and as she spoke she knew that what she was saying was true.

It would not be right. Not for Alex, not for her, and, most importantly of all, not for those whose welfare, whose working lives, whose homes were his responsibility.

In a perfect world all humans would be equal in one another's eyes, equal to each other, but in an imperfect one, filled with human frailties and vulnerabilities, it was different.

Mollie took a deep breath and made the biggest and

most important decision—after acknowledging her love for Alex—that she hoped she would have to make in her life.

'No, you can't do that,' she told him firmly. 'Our son has a right to make his own choice as to whether or not he inherits from you, Alex. *We* can't make that decision for him.'

'Our *son*?' he protested.

'Our son,' Mollie agreed.

'But we haven't... You aren't...' Alex began.

But Mollie stopped him, wrapping her arms lovingly around him as she agreed, 'No, I'm not...not yet. But I could be soon if you...' Putting her lips close to his ear, she whispered something to him.

'Only if you promise to marry me,' Alex mock threatened her.

Mollie laughed.

'Try and stop me,' she teased him, adding huskily, 'And try and stop this as well, if you can...'

'I can't,' Alex admitted rawly minutes later, when she had finished kissing him. 'Oh, Mollie, Mollie, I love you so much,' he told her thickly as his hand slid down to cup her breast.

Languorously Mollie watched him. His hand looked so dark and strong against the paler, softer flesh of her breast, but he was the one who was trembling as he caressed the tight point of her nipple.

A sharp quiver ran across her body, her stomach muscles tensing. 'The medics told me I had to bring you home and let you rest. They warned me that you were suffering from shock,' Alex protested as Mollie lifted her head and started to kiss his shoulder.

'Was that why you brought me here to the Queen's

bed? If you wanted me to rest, you shouldn't have got into bed with me,' Mollie told him mock severely.

'I didn't have any option,' Alex told her ruefully. 'You were so traumatised that you didn't want to let me go. You kept begging me to stay with you.'

'Mmm...' Mollie wriggled potently against him as he gave in to the temptation to kiss the dark, hard peak of her breast and then to take it into his mouth and caress it slowly and lovingly.

'Did I beg you to take your clothes off as well?' she asked him archly, not waiting for an answer as she gasped softly and arched her back, clasping the back of his head to hold his mouth even closer to her body.

'No, *that* was my own idea,' he admitted when he had finally and reluctantly relinquished her.

Mollie blushed as she looked down at her sensitised and very obviously aroused flesh. The whole of her body ached and tingled. Instinctively she pressed her body, her sex, closer to Alex, shivering in mute pleasure as he sensed her need and moved his hand down to cover and then touch her, his fingers delicately parting the outer layers of flesh, stroking, caressing, making her wantonly aware of the warm moistness of her inner womanhood and how much it ached for the erotic heat of his caress.

'Did you really write my name in flour?' she heard Alex asking her gruffly through the sensual daze of pleasure that was flooding her.

'What...? Oh, yes... Who told you about that?' she gasped, before moaning protestingly, 'Alex, I don't want to *talk* any more. I want...'

'Sylvie told me,' he informed her. 'She said she

took that to mean you loved me. And to think I had begun to despair of that girl's intelligence. She's completely restored my faith in her. With that kind of acute perception she's bound to make good...'

Mollie gave the ghost of a small moaned laugh before her whole body started to shudder with the quivers of pleasure darting through it as Alex began to trace a pathway of delicate, delicious kisses all over her body, starting at her throat and making his way with leisurely but determined insistence over her breasts and past her waist, pausing to slip his hands beneath her as he circled her navel.

Closing her eyes, Mollie moaned, 'Alex, Alex, Alex,' shuddering in aching delight when he parted her thighs and reaching out to caress him in return.

His skin, his body felt so good beneath her touch, so warm and alive, so, so right. *He* felt so right.

Earlier today, contemplating her own death, the strongest emotion she had felt—stronger even than her fear—had been her joy in having known him, in having loved him, and her anguish at knowing she might never be like this with him again.

Very gently she pushed him slightly away from her, smiling lovingly up at him through the darkness as she shook her head and whispered, 'No. Not yet. I want to do this first...'

She heard him gasp and then felt him tense as she touched his body, caressed it, first with her fingertips and then her mouth in exactly the same way that he had caressed hers.

Like him, she made her way lingeringly and lovingly downwards, pausing to tease lightly at the flat hardness of his belly with her finger and then her tongue-tip, circling his navel, biting gently at his skin, stroking her hands slowly over his thighs, knowing that the tremors she could feel beneath her weren't just generated by *his* sexual tension, that *she*, too, was acutely responsive to what she was building between them.

The scent of his body, his arousal, filled the heated soft air of the room, and Mollie instinctively started to breathe more slowly and more deeply, reacting sensually to the silent, subtle messages of his sex. Around them the pheromone-laden air whispered silken promises every bit as erotic as the whispered words that passed from Mollie's lips to Alex's skin, and back again from his lips to her.

This time *he* was the one to chant her name in helpless adoration and need as her fingers daringly stroked the hard male heat of him before she slowly bent her head and caressed him intimately with exquisite tender care.

She felt his body tense and then shudder, and then he was reaching for her, dragging her urgently upwards, covering her body with his.

Her eyes filling with loving, emotional tears, Mollie looked into his face and saw with a sharp, bittersweet surge of love that Alex's eyes, too, were damp.

'I don't know what I'd have done if I'd lost you,' he whispered thickly against her throat. 'What I'd *do* if ever I lost you.'

'I was so afraid,' Mollie told him. 'All I could think was that I might never see you again and be glad that at least I'd had...known...you,' she told him truthfully.

'Known me...' Alex murmured, smiling at her as he brushed the silken hair off her face.

Gravely Mollie met the look in his eyes.

'Known you here,' she told him quietly, touching her heart, and then adding in an even quieter voice as she touched the other, physical feminine heart of her body, 'And known you here...

'I want you, Alex,' she whispered urgently to him, drawing him closer to her. 'I want you so much... Now...now...now,' she chanted urgently, closing her eyes with a sobbed gasp of pure joy as she opened herself to him and felt him beginning to move within her, picking up the rhythm of the words she had just chanted.

'Alex. Oh, Alex.'

Instinctively she wrapped herself around him, using her arms and her legs to hold him closer, knowing with pure, soul-deep feminine instinct that this was the right time for her to conceive his child, and that this child, their child, would be conceived not just in love and joy but with a deep, deep sense of mutual gratitude for the gift not just of his or her life but of their own.

All around them the house settled down into a contented peaceful silence, its future safe and secure, as if it sensed the creation of a new generation destined to protect, love and cherish it.

EPILOGUE

MOLLIE made a small *moue* as her new husband carefully picked the fresh rose petals from her hair.

They had been married an hour earlier in the small consecrated chapel of the house which had been the St Otel family seat at the time of the Wars of the Roses.

The austerity of the massive stone-built fortification that was the northern castle was such that it was not appealing as a family home, even though the apartment which the charitable trust had allocated there for the family's use was relatively comfortable, but it was the tradition that the Earls of St Otel married there, and Mollie had insisted that it was a tradition which she had no intention of breaking.

When Alex had given her a wry look she had told him, 'Might bring us bad luck.'

'The bad luck will be getting married there,' he said dryly. 'It will be freezing cold—the walls are at least ten feet thick—and it's bound to rain.'

He had been wrong—on both counts—and if the expressions on the faces of Alex's employees and tenants—all of whom had been invited to participate in their wedding celebrations—were anything to go by they had been as thrilled with Mollie's choice of venue as she had herself.

She had worn a very simple plain dress. Simple and plain but horrendously expensive, requiring metre upon metre of impossibly expensive duchesse satin, but the effect had been truly worth every hour she had spent patiently having it fitted. The slightly medieval style of the gown discreetly masked the beginnings of the small delicate bulge which was rounding out her stomach.

'It's quite a tradition for St Otel brides to produce premature babies,' Alex had told her loftily when she had confided to him that their first child was going to arrive well in advance of their first wedding anniversary.

Mollie had giggled.

'This one will certainly be that. I doubt he or she's going to let us celebrate our first *six months* of marriage before making its arrival.'

'Tongues will wag,' Alex had told her, tongue-in-cheek. 'They'll say you tricked me into marriage...'

'No. *I'll* say that *you* seduced me into it,' Mollie had retorted back.

'Ah, yes, of course, in my role as the wicked villain of the piece...'

'Claiming his droit du seigneur,' Mollie had agreed.

They had still been laughing when he had started to kiss her.

Laughter and kisses featured strongly in their lives, and she intended to see that they went on doing so, Mollie decided as she smiled up into her new husband's eyes.

It was, both of them agreed, the icing on the cake and very good news indeed that Alex's caring negotiations had resulted in the travellers agreeing to move voluntarily to the designated site. They and Alex were all agreed they would be far more comfortable there over the coming winter months.

Less damage than had been feared had been done to the wood, and Ran and Alex had organised a team of helpers to clean it up, comprising youngsters both from the town and the camp—a co-operative and peace-making joint effort.

'It's a pity that Sylvie couldn't be here,' Mollie murmured.

'Mmm…I know. But, as she said herself, now that she's got herself settled with her degree course, she's going to have to work hard to make up the time she's missed…'

'I know, but to decide to finish her education in America…' She sighed.

'It's for the best,' Alex reminded her. 'There's bound to be some publicity over the case when Wayne eventually goes before a court, and with Sylvie out of the country she can avoid that—and any potential disruption from her mother.'

'She just looked so unhappy when we saw her off at Heathrow.'

'We'll give her a couple of months to settle in and then we'll fly over and visit her,' Alex offered.

'I didn't expect Ran to turn up like that either, did you?'

'What, you mean to see Sylvie off at Heathrow? No…that was…surprising,' Alex agreed.

'Sylvie was quite put out about it. She said he'd only done it because he wanted to make sure she *was* actually leaving the country.'

'Yes. There's quite a lot of antagonism between the pair of them, which is odd when you think that when

Sylvie first knew Ran she used to follow him around like a little puppy.

'She was a lot younger then, of course—only a girl—and her mother disapproved most strongly and told my father that he was to tell Ran to keep away from her. She didn't want *her* daughter mixing with the estate workers, apparently.'

'She *is* rather a snob,' Mollie interjected wryly. 'I know the first time we met she virtually cross-questioned me about my background.'

'Mmm... The joke of the whole thing is that in reality Ran probably has a longer and far more aristocratic pedigree than *any* of us—if, like my stepmother, you're impressed by such things...'

'Has he?' Mollie looked questioningly at her husband. 'But he doesn't have a title or...'

'No title, no, but he *is* still descended from one of the grandest families in the land! Enough about Ran and my wretched stepmama, though. We have far more important and...interesting matters to discuss...'

'Oh, Alex,' Mollie murmured lovingly.

'Oh, Alex what?' Alex challenged her teasingly, his eyes lighting up as he whispered the words in the same husky, broken-voiced way she used when they made love.

'Alex, not now,' Mollie protested mock primly, only to find her protest melting beneath the passion of his kiss as she amended huskily, 'Well, at least...not yet...'

Look out for Syvlie and Ran's story— coming soon.

Big, brash and brazen...

THE

AUSTRALIANS

Stories of romance Australian-style guaranteed to
fulfill that sense of adventure!

This August, look for
Heartthrob for Hire
by Miranda Lee

Roy Fitzsimmons had those rugged good looks that women
would die for. So why was he pursuing Kate? Kate Reynolds was
more at home in the boardroom than the bedroom. Then an
overheard telephone conversation gave her some clues. Could
Roy be hiring himself out to lonely women? He *seemed* too
genuine to be a gigolo, but Kate decided to put her theory to the
test and offer to pay Roy to pose as her lover.... But would
he accept?

*The Wonder from Down Under: where spirited women win
the hearts of Australia's most independent men!*

Available August 1998 at your favorite retail outlet.

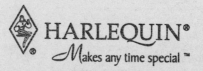

HARLEQUIN®
Makes any time special ™

Take 2 bestselling love stories FREE

Plus get a FREE surprise gift!

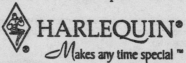

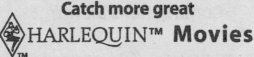

 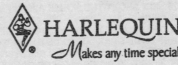

Coming Next Month

HARLEQUIN PRESENTS®

THE BEST HAS JUST GOTTEN BETTER!

#1971 THE RELUCTANT HUSBAND Lynne Graham
Unbeknown to Frankie, her marriage to Santino had never
been annulled—and now he was intending to claim the
wedding night they'd never had! But Santino hadn't
bargained on falling for Frankie all over again....

#1972 INHERITED: ONE NANNY Emma Darcy
(Nanny Wanted!)
When Beau Prescott heard he'd inherited a nanny with his
grandfather's estate, he imagined Margaret Stowe to be a
starchy spinster. But she turned out to be a beautiful young
woman. Just what situation had he inherited here?

#1973 MARRIAGE ON THE REBOUND Michelle Reid
Rafe Danvers had always acted as if he despised Shaan; he
even persuaded his stepbrother to jilt her on her wedding
day. Yet suddenly Rafe wanted to proclaim her to the world
as his wife—and Shaan wanted to know why....

#1974 TEMPORARY PARENTS Sara Wood
Laura had sworn never to see her ex-lover, Max, again. But
cocooned in a cliff-top cottage with him, watching him play
daddy to her small niece and nephew, it was all too easy to
pretend she and Max were together again....

#1975 MAN ABOUT THE HOUSE Alison Kelly
(Man Talk!)
Brett had decided women were unreliable, and right now he
wanted to be single. Or so he thought—until he agreed to
house-sit for his mother, and discovered another house-
sitter already in residence—the gorgeous Joanna!

#1976 TEMPTING LUCAS Catherine Spencer
Emily longed to tell Lucas about the consequences of their
one-night stand eleven years ago, and that she still loved
him. But she was determined that if they ever made love
again, it would be he who'd come to her....